"Breaking right," came the call from Wilde.

"Rolling in."

Anderson aimed the nose of the aircraft at the center of the fires. In the flash of the rockets and then the burning of the hootches, he had seen men running, many of them armed. Now he felt the aircraft shudder and saw flashes of brightness as Sadler fired the rockets.

"Break! Break!"

Anderson realized that he was staring at the target and diving down into it. He pulled the collective and pushed the cyclic and they began a turning climb. Behind him the machine guns began to hammer as the chief and doorgun opened fire.

He came around again as the enemy started to shoot back. Strobing flashes marked the enemy soldiers. Sadler fired the last of their rockets. Streams of green and white tracers came at the chopper—slamming into the aircraft.

Then Wilde rolled in with his mini guns firing on both sides . . .

WINGS
OVER
NAM

CHOPPER PILOT

ALSO BY CAT BRANIGAN

Wings Over Nam #2:
The Wild Weasels

Wings Over Nam #3:
Linebacker

forthcoming from
POPULAR LIBRARY

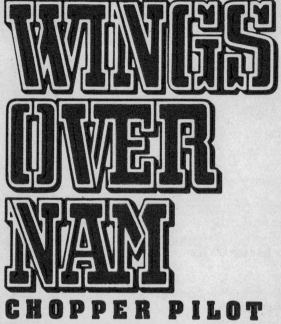

WINGS OVER NAM

CHOPPER PILOT

Cat Branigan

POPULAR LIBRARY

An Imprint of Warner Books, Inc.

A Warner Communications Company

Popular Library books are published by
Warner Books, Inc.
666 Fifth Avenue
New York, N.Y. 10103

 A Warner Communications Company

Printed in the United States of America

First Printing: June, 1989

10 9 8 7 6 5 4 3 2 1

PROLOGUE

WHEN David Alexander Anderson was a little boy he spent his Saturday afternoons sitting in a darkened theater watching the exploits of John Wayne as he single-handedly fought all of America's wars. Ten years later he sat in a dimly lit bunker that smelled of dirt, blood, sweat, and gunpowder, and wondered where all the glamour of Hollywood had gone (if it had ever existed at all). A young man, barely nineteen and just out of the Army's Warrant Officer Flight Training, Anderson hadn't had the time to learn that war was not the glamorous, glorious thing that John Wayne and his imitators had led him to believe. He was still caught up in the pride of wearing a uniform that said U.S. ARMY above the pocket.

Anderson was tall and skinny, weighing no more than a hundred and forty pounds, and he had short-cropped brown hair and blue-gray eyes. He had dodged the draft by joining the Army and then taken various tests that qualified him for

I

all of the Army's schools except the Staff and War College. He missed that because he had no college degree. Anderson opted for flight school when some sage along the way told him, "You don't walk through Vietnam, you fly over it."

Anderson took basic training at Fort Polk and was then given orders to Fort Wolters, Texas, the Army's primary helicopter school. The Army, in its infinite wisdom, had decided that because of the nature of the war in Vietnam it needed more helicopter pilots, and had expanded the program. Unfortunately, they couldn't expand the training facilities with equal speed, and Anderson found himself with little to occupy his time except staying out of the way. He spent his days sleeping late and dodging work, and filled his evenings at the post theater, where John Wayne was still fighting America's celluloid wars. The idyllic existence lasted for several weeks, until Anderson began preflight training. Then it was up before five, with classes scheduled from eight until five or six, tests weekly (sometimes daily), inspections, extra duties, studying, and weekend formations. He was back in the real Army.

Four weeks later, he was moved to flight school, which was on the "hill" (Anderson learned that every military post had a hill), but now the class time was broken up by time on the flight line.

Flying helicopters wasn't much different from flying airplanes, except that both hands and both feet were busy with the controls at all times (not to mention that the collective, the stick that changed the pitch of the rotorblades, also held the throttle). Every time pitch was added or subtracted, the throttle had to be twisted to add power or subtract it. And each of those movements meant that the pilot had to use one of the pedals to maintain straight flight, and, finally, that a correction had to be made with the cyclic to make sure that the airspeed remained constant.

Hovering was a different matter. It meant that the pilot had to anticipate the aircraft and make the changes before anything happened to throw off the hover. One of Anderson's instructors told him to think about the movement but not make it. "What happens is that thinking about it makes you move your hand slightly and that usually is enough of a control correction."

He and the other trainees spent their time learning to fly and then learning helicopter maintenance, tactics, how to call in artillery, and a hundred other military subjects. The days turned into weeks, the weeks into months, and the next thing Anderson knew he had orders for Vietnam. It was after they got the orders that they finished training. It seemed to be a backward way of doing things.

Anderson spent his leave trying to ignore what he had come to believe was impending doom. While most of his high school buddies were now freshmen in college with nothing more horrible than midterms facing them, Anderson was about to cross the Big Pond to learn if the Vietcong could shoot straight. He dated several girls while on leave, having as much fun as possible, but not mentioning to them that he was on his way to Vietnam. He just told them that he was home on leave from the Army. None of them asked about Vietnam.

The only exception was Susan Webb. He told her everything, including that he wasn't happy about the orders. "I noticed one thing," he told her one night. "When I first entered flight school, most of the guys couldn't wait to get to Vietnam. But as time progressed, and it looked like they weren't going to get the war over before we graduated, they decided that it might not be the great adventure they thought. I don't think too many of them are all that excited about this."

"And you?" she asked.

He didn't have an answer to the question. No one had ever asked his opinion. The Army had told him that he was going, and that had ended all discussion about it.

Now, sitting in a bunker at Cu Chi, he still didn't have an opinion about the politics of the war. He did have feelings, however, and those were the reason he was in the bunker, a metal file in one hand and a 2.75-inch rocket in the other. The serial numbers had to be removed before they could go on their mission, because it was not sanctioned through official channels.

Anderson wiped the sweat from his forehead, using the sleeve of his jungle fatigues. That was another thing no one had told him about Vietnam. It was hot and humid, but not like the sticky nights of the Midwest. This was an oppressive heat with a high humidity, and the frequent rains did nothing to break the heat. They made it worse, adding to the water in the atmosphere.

In fact, in his several weeks in Vietnam, Anderson had found little to like about the country and a great deal to hate. From the people who wouldn't support them to those who shot at them. From the government that was subtly corrupt to the local officials who were blatantly corrupt. From the Army that refused to stand and fight to the soldiers who tried to sell their weapons for an illegal ride to Saigon. It was a sorry, sickening place, and Anderson tried to have nothing to do with the South Vietnamese.

He finished with the rocket and gave it to one of the others in the bunker with him. The man placed it in the rear, where no one would be inclined to take it, and got him another. They worked in relative silence, the only sounds the scrapping of the files on the metal and the noise of helicopters operating on the airfield half a mile away.

ONE

AS they sat hovering over the rubberized helipad in the UH-1D helicopter, David Alexander Anderson did not know that the Vietcong were not the most dangerous enemy in Vietnam. It was the Flaming Mimi. And he didn't know that he would meet the Flaming Mimi in a matter of hours, but would not see the Vietcong for weeks.

As the Huey settled into a choking cloud of red dust that obscured everything nearby, the nineteen-year-old Anderson was ready to battle the enemy. He was ready to leap into the jaws of death to fight communist aggression in South Vietnam, just as the instructors in flight school had taught him. A thin, tall man who was already trying to grow a mustache, he sat strapped on the canvas troopseat, ignoring the afternoon glare, the heat and humidity that swirled about in the dust, and wiped the sweat beading his forehead onto the sleeve of his bright-green jungle fatigues.

When the helicopter had touched the pad and the cloud

began to dissipate, Anderson stared across the road at a series of wooden buildings with tin roofs. Shacks protected by green sandbags, some of which were spilling their contents, they were lined up side by side, looking like British soldiers waiting for the Americans to gun them down.

For a kid from the Midwest, used to a house that had indoor plumbing and all-night electricity, it didn't look like much. He hoped that it was the supply area and that the living quarters were hidden somewhere behind the shacks. In front of them he could see a single flagpole with a pile of suitcases and equipment beside it.

The pilot turned in his seat, put an arm up on the back of the armor, and pushed the boom mike out of the way. "Crew chief will get your gear," he shouted over the roar of the turbine. He pointed through the Plexiglas, toward the building nearest the flagpole. "You're supposed to report to the Orderly Room. Major Fox is expecting you."

Anderson unbuckled the seat belt and jumped out. He stood next to the Huey, blinking rapidly. The smell of JP-4, the fuel used by the helicopters, filled the air . . . that, and an odor he would later learn was burning shit. The water table was so high that the only way to get rid of the residue of the latrines was to mix it with kerosene and burn it.

He ducked slightly and ran to the edge of the pad. He stopped there and turned in time to see the crew chief grab his duffel bag, flipping it to the ground. Anderson ran across the road and stopped at the flagpole, looking down at the collection of suitcases, duffel bags, and a single, bolt-action rifle.

As the crew chief approached, Anderson asked, "What now?"

The man, dressed in jungle fatigues that had faded to gray, boots that had only a trace of black on them, and a canvas-covered chicken plate, shrugged. "Hell, sir, that's your problem. I'm just supposed to drop this shit here. You're the officer." He whirled then and ran back toward the Huey.

Anderson turned in a complete circle, like a man who'd lost his car in a huge parking lot, and wondered what in the hell he was doing in Vietnam. So far it had been nothing more than a nightmare of processing through the Army's long chain that made sure he got to Vietnam without getting lost. He stood there for a moment, trying to get his bearings. No one had seemed happy to see him, although they all had welcomed him to Vietnam. Not exactly the words that he had longed to hear.

He wiped the sweat from his face again and headed toward the Orderly Room. Inside there was a specialist sitting behind a worn wooden desk that had at one time been painted OD green. The man, not much older than Anderson, wore sweat-soaked jungle fatigues with the sleeves rolled up halfway between the elbow and the shoulder. As Anderson approached, the man said, "Let me see your orders, sir."

Anderson ripped a copy off the top of the stack and handed it over without a word. Until that point, everyone in the Army had outranked him because no one was lower than a trainee, whether he was in basic or flight school. He still wasn't used to them being polite to him.

The specialist scanned the orders, dropped them onto a stack of paper, then nodded at the other two men sitting across the room. "Have a seat and the major will be with you in just a moment."

Like Anderson, the other two men were warrant officers, both looking as if they'd just arrived. They were wearing bright-green jungle fatigues that had no insignia on them. Anderson didn't really recognize them, although one might have been in his company in flight school. The platoons had been clannish, and he had never really met most of the men in the other platoons.

He sat down on the end of the broken-down settee that was shoved against one plywood wall. The vinyl was ripped in a couple of places, and no one had bothered to fix it. For a moment he stared out the door, into the bright sunlight. Beyond the flagpole was his gear, still sitting there, and beyond that was a dusty road used occasionally by trucks and jeeps. He watched the road for a moment, then looked up at the ceiling fan spinning slowly overhead. Somehow this was not what he had expected of Vietnam, but then he wasn't sure exactly what he had expected.

There was a noise to the left, and Major Fox opened the door to the air-conditioned office. Fox was a small, thin man with jet-black hair and a deep tropical tan. His jungle fatigues were fresh and starched and looked tailored. The insignia was subdued, in blacks and deep coppers, and there wasn't a thread or wrinkle anywhere.

"You gentlemen may join me now. And close the door." He disappeared again.

Anderson shrugged at the other two, stood, and entered the office. It was cold, had walls paneled in plywood stained a deep brown, no windows, and a piece of worn carpeting in front of a battered desk thrust into the corner. Fox had already seated himself and was working again.

The three new officers formed a line on the carpeting. Before Anderson could speak, one of the others said, "Sir, Warrant Officer Charles Crawford reporting as ordered."

Fox dropped his pencil and returned the salute, then turned to the next man, Morgan, letting him run through the ritual. Anderson followed, and when they had finished, Fox gestured at a duplicate of the settee in the Orderly Room and said, "Take a seat, gentlemen, and tell me a little about yourselves."

While the other two men talked, Anderson looked around the office. There was a table set close to one wall with six chairs around it, like some kind of a conference area. There were a couple of captured weapons hanging on the walls, looking like mounted game fish. An American flag stood in one corner.

When Anderson's turn came, he wasn't sure what to say. He'd graduated from high school, gone immediately into the Army, and then to flight school. There hadn't been much choice in the matter, given his circumstances at home. There hadn't been money for college, and the Army had seemed an easy way to finance an education, but Anderson hadn't really thought things through when he volunteered for flight school. Helicopter pilots weren't doing too well, and the day the VC and NVA shot down fifty Hueys in the A Shau Valley, twenty-three men had quit flight school. Anderson wondered if he should have been one of them, especially now.

He tried to think of things that he was proud of, but suddenly, in the adult world of real war, everything sounded juvenile, if not outright childish. There had been no chance to accomplish anything. He stumbled around for a couple of minutes, jumping from his high-school experiences to his Army training and back again. Finally, feeling his face grow red with embarrassment, he said, "I guess that's about all, sir."

When the interview was finished, Fox had learned very little about the new men and really didn't care about it, because he was there to fight a war and not win a popularity contest. He took them out into the company area, and Anderson learned that this wasn't, as he had hoped, some kind of supply area. This was the living quarters. There were several rows of dilapidated one-story buildings. Around the outer walls of each one were stacks of sandbags, about three feet high. The wooden outer walls extended only slightly higher than that and were then screened to the eaves. Corrugated tin formed a peaked roof. Outside most was a tower holding a fifty-five-gallon drum that was filled with water for each of the hootches. There were wooden walks between the hootches, made of two-by-twelves on their sides linked by two-by-tens. Wires were strung everywhere, looking like an afterthought that had been blown up. Running down the center of the area was a series of sandbagged bunkers, covered with PSP, fifty-five-gallon drums set on end, and another layer of PSP.

Anderson had seen pictures of third world countries where the living conditions seemed better. Bushmen in the heart of Africa had better living conditions. Men in prison rioted if their living conditions weren't considered adequate. If this had been a prison, the riot would have broken out months before.

They entered one of the hootches, in search of the platoon leaders. Captain Davis was sitting in the large "dayroom" area of one hootch. The floors were dirty, bare plywood.

Overhead hung the canopy from a parachute flare, and through the center of it was suspended a ceiling fan that wasn't working. The canopy was so dirty that it looked gray, and it had probably been there since the hootch was built.

Fox left two of the new men with Davis and then waved at Anderson. "You'll be with the Second Platoon. Captain Brown is probably in the club."

Anderson stood in the doorway, looking past the bar, at the two huge floor fans that roared in the corners, creating a hot breeze. Fox entered, motioned toward Brown, and when the captain joined them said, "I think we'll assign this one to you. Find him a place to stay."

Brown turned and set a can of beer on the bar. He was a tall, burly man who looked to be twenty-five or -six. He had light hair, a rounded face, and a large nose. His eyes were dark and his skin tanned. Unlike Fox, Brown's uniform was not tailored, was not starched, and was sweat-stained.

He seemed annoyed at the interruption but said, "Follow me."

Fox deserted Anderson then. Brown led him through the area to a hootch and told him to wait in the dayroom. There was a tiny black-and-white TV sitting in a niche built into a bar that filled one corner. The top of the bar was covered with green floor tile, and the sides with white bathroom tile. A number of the pieces were broken or chipped, and more than one was missing.

One man, extremely tall and thin, was sitting in a ragged lawn chair watching a rerun of *The Dean Martin Show*. Off to one side was a white refrigerator. Someone had scrawled on the front, "Keep your fucking hands off my beer."

Opposite it, in the other corner, was a sink with a dirty mirror, and above that was a shelf containing empty beer bottles. Anderson took it all in, shook his head, and sat down to watch Dean Martin.

A couple of minutes later, Brown was back. "You'll stay here." He pointed to a room to one side and said, "You can store your gear and I'll see you later." Without another word he disappeared, probably on his way back to the club and his beer.

Alone, Anderson walked out to the flagpole where he had last seen his gear. He separated his duffel bag and flight helmet from the pile and carried them back to the hootch. He found that one of the gray wall lockers contained clothes but that the other was empty. He stored his gear by dumping it in the bottom of the locker and slamming the door. Then he crawled up on the top bunk, which had no sheets or pillow, and went to sleep.

It was dark when someone shook him awake. He opened his eyes, stared into the night. A single light burned behind the man's shape, so that Anderson couldn't make out his features.

"You Anderson?"

"Yeah."

"Meeting in the club, now. You got to go. Major Fox is expecting you."

Anderson sat up. He was dizzy, his head hurt, and his mouth tasted like mud. He was bathed in sweat that soaked his shirt and the waistband of his jungle fatigues. He swung his feet over the side of the bunk and gripped the edge with both hands. For an instant he sat there and wished that he hadn't gone to sleep, because he now felt worse than before. He hadn't even taken the time to remove his boots.

Finally, he dropped to the floor and then stumbled through the company area until he blundered into the club. He entered through the side and saw nearly two dozen wicker tables and twice that many chairs scattered around the room. There were a couple of slot machines against one wall. The bar was crowded with officers trying to get a final drink before Fox called the meeting to order. He stood on a raised stage in one corner, a couple of spotlights shining on him. He waited until nearly everyone was seated and the talking had died, and then he started.

"First things first. Garay, you want bourbon or scotch?"

Garay stood up and walked to the stage, grinning. Like almost everyone in the room, he was a young man, tall and thin. He had sandy hair and a long, thin face. He wore jungle fatigues that were faded nearly gray, and still wore his pistol in an Old West style holster that had loops for six rounds on the holster, but no weapon in it.

As he stepped up on the stage, he said, "I'll take a scotch." He waited while the bartender poured a double shot and brought it forward. As he handed the drink to Garay, another officer stood and struck a match. Garay held out the drink so that the top of the scotch could be set on fire, creating a Flaming Mimi.

Fox announced, "Garay passed his AC checkride today. Tomorrow he leaves the ranks of the Peter Pilots and joins that of the big boys." He gestured with his right hand. "Drink up."

Garay put the glass to his lips and drank quickly. When he finished, there was a swirl of fire in the bottom of the glass that brought wild cheering. Someone yelled, "Now the fucking new guys. Now the fucking new guys." The rest of the men took up the chant until it drowned out all other sounds, including the roaring of the huge fans and the beat of rotorblades coming from the airfield across the road.

Fox pointed at the new guys, including Anderson, and said, "Gentlemen, if you'll join me."

Each man was asked what he wanted. Anderson opted for bourbon, his drink of choice. Since learning nearly three months ago that the drinking age on military bases had no relation to the drinking age in the states surrounding them, he had been drinking bourbon. Not because he liked it especially, but because he knew that he could drink bourbon and Coke and no one would laugh at the order.

The bartender brought the three drinks and Fox set each of them on fire. Morgan and Crawford grabbed theirs quickly, threw back their heads, and drank. As Anderson brought his to his lips, he snorted through his nose, blowing out the fire, but he swallowed the bourbon in a single gulp.

"Cheat! Cheat! The fucking new guy cheated. Make him do it again," screamed the man who had started the chant.

Again Fox pointed, and the bartender rushed another shot glass forward, this time filled to the brim. Fox used his lighter to set it on fire and handed it carefully to Anderson.

Now Anderson hesitated and heard someone warn, "You better drink it before it gets too hot."

The advice sounded good, so Anderson drank it, but there was no fire left in the bottom of the glass. Fox shrugged and said, "Again."

The third attempt was another failure. He swallowed the bourbon quickly and held the glass aloft, as if that would start the fire again. Everyone began shouting for a fourth, and that resulted in a fourth failure.

Now Anderson was beginning to get dizzy. He hadn't eaten all day, had flown halfway around the world in the last week, and, even after the nap, was tired. The four double shots of straight bourbon were beginning to get to him. The room had become fuzzy and the lights seemed to have halos around them. His stomach vibrated, and he wondered if he was going to be sick.

Fox didn't say a word. He signaled the bartender, who brought the bottle.

"Hey," shouted one of the men, "the fucking new guy is getting a lot of free drinks."

"Yeah, he's not such a dummy."

"You going to make him do it right, Major?"

Fox didn't answer, he just poured another double shot and waited while someone set it on fire. "You better get this one right, because I don't think you had better drink any more tonight."

But Anderson didn't do it right. He came close, but there was no fire when he finished. Fox clapped him on the shoulder and said, "A noble effort, if all in vain. Have a seat."

Anderson dropped to the floor like he had been shot. He

began to giggle helplessly as the rest of the officers cheered wildly.

"What a cheap drunk. Too bad he's not female."

Fox glanced down at Anderson, then said, "Okay, with the preliminaries out of the way, let's get on to the business at hand. Captain Miller, you had the C and C today. What'd you see?"

Anderson watched the first few minutes of the officer's call, listening to the list of what had been done right and what had been done wrong. There was talk of sloppy formation flying, late takeoffs from the LZ, and too much chatter on the radios. Anderson tried to listen to it all, but remembered almost nothing about it the next day.

The next thing Anderson knew, someone was shaking him awake and asking, again, "You Anderson?"

He was hit with a feeling of déjà vu that was quickly replaced by a feeling of sickness. His head spun, and he lay quietly, refusing to move. He blinked at the bright light blazing in through the open door of the hootch, and finally said, "Yeah."

"You need to get to supply and draw a weapon and the rest of your flight gear. You got a checkride in an hour." The man spun and ran out before Anderson had a chance to ask him any of the dozen questions that filled his mind. Then he tried to sit up and felt like he was going to throw up. Too much booze too fast, without any food to absorb it.

"How the fuck am I supposed to fly?"

He forced himself to get out of bed. Again, he'd failed to get out of his clothes, and he still had no sheets or pillow, but he'd managed to take off his boots.

He stood there and stripped out of his dirty uniform, wishing that he had time to take a shower. His skin itched with the dried sweat and dirt. He stumbled into the front room, and then to the sink. He tried a faucet and found a thin trickle of water. He turned it off and returned to his room, so that he could get a toothbrush and toothpaste. He brushed his teeth and then used the lukewarm water to shave. The razor dragged, and he cut himself a couple of times. His hands were shaking and his head throbbed. Flying was the last thing he wanted to do.

Dressed, he stepped into the morning sun. It seemed to be hotter than the sun in the United States. It seemed brighter too. He squinted up at it and then followed the wooden walk until he came to a long, low building of corrugated metal. There was a huge sliding door that was open. There was a small sign to one side that read COMPANY SUPPLY.

Anderson entered and stopped at the waist-high wooden counter. He could see little, only a couple of shelves filled with clothes and another floor fan that blew warm air in his face.

A short, fat man appeared and leaned on the counter. "What you want?"

"I was told to come over and collect my flight gear and a weapon."

"Yeah, fine." The man bent down and pulled a couple of forms from under the counter. "Fill 'em out." He slapped a pen down next to the forms and then vanished. He returned, dropped a bundle of clothes on the counter, and retreated again. He came back with another arm-load of equipment, put a pistol on top of it all, and then plucked the forms from the counter.

Anderson watched the man add the nomenclature for each item to the forms and, when he finished, sign them. He gathered the equipment and carried it back to his hootch. With the checkride now only fifteen minutes off, he didn't have time to do anything except leave the gear piled on his bunk.

Anderson hurried out to the helipad where the chopper waited, its rotor spinning. There were no machine guns in the doors, and the only passenger was the instructor, Weiss, who was in command of the checkride. As Anderson strapped himself in, the aircraft picked up to a hover, spun, and then began to move toward the runway, creating a giant cloud of red dust in its wake.

The checkride was little more than a reintroduction to the aircraft. It had been nearly two months since Anderson had flown. While the other new guys waited on the ground, Anderson and the instructor went out to try autorotations, normal approaches, and run-throughs of some of the emergency procedures. It took less than an hour, and then Anderson found himself back on the ground.

Before he got out, he keyed the mike on the intercom and asked, "How'd I do?"

The instructor was writing on a form. He glanced at Anderson and said, "Fine. Just fine. Little rusty on a couple of things, but you've been down for a while."

"Now I'll get scheduled with the flight?"

"No. First there is a combat-assault checkride before you're released to the flight."

"When will that be?"

"Couple of days. They'll let you know."

Anderson climbed out, nodded at the last of the new guys who now had to fly. As the man climbed into the cockpit, Anderson dropped to the ground and watched the chopper take off.

Instead of returning to Cu Chi after the checkrides, De-Weiss announced, "We're going to fly into Saigon, get you boys a look at the airport there and Hotel Three—that's the name of the heliport."

All three of the new guys were plugged into the intercom system so that they could hear everything the instructor said. One of them was flying as his copilot. Luck of the draw had put Anderson in the back, on the red-canvas troopseat, where all he could do was look outside of the cargo compartment.

They left the airfield, heading due south until they crossed over a highway. It was a two-lane paved road. The jungle on either side had been cut way back so that the enemy would have trouble ambushing truck convoys. The greens were deep and vibrant. There was a small hamlet tucked under a growth of trees—mud hootches, some with tin roofs and others with thatch.

As they reached the highway, they turned to the east, following the south side of the road. "We follow the standard rules of the road here. You fly on the same side of the road as you'd drive on if you were foolish enough to be on the ground."

Anderson looked out the door. The trees had faded away, and he was looking at a large, flat plain that stretched as far as he could see. Sunlight reflected from it, and he realized that it was a huge marsh or swamp. There was plenty of vegetation hiding the water.

It seemed that only a few minutes had passed. They dropped out of the sky until they were low-leveling. De-Weiss was on the intercom again. "We have to keep below the flight paths at Tan Son Nhut."

They shot through a gap in a tree line and then popped up to five hundred feet. DeWeiss switched to the radio and called the tower. They were given permission to land and told to park on the grass near the chain-link fence that separated Hotel Three from the rest of Tan Son Nhut.

They made the landing, coming down over a series of low buildings, aiming for a square of green land. As soon as they landed and DeWeiss had shut down the engine, he stripped off his helmet, hanging it on the hook behind his seat.

"Gentlemen," he said, "you're in for a real treat now. We're going to the Gunfighter's Club."

TWO

THEY left Hotel Three after closing up the helicopter. They couldn't lock the doors, but they did shut them all. They put their helmets under the troopseat, where they were out of sight, and carried their pistols.

"Can't go walking around the base armed," DeWeiss told them. He pulled his fatigue jacket out so that it covered his pistol belt, hiding the weapon.

They walked past the terminal and down a short road, and turned toward a large, single-story building.

"That," said DeWeiss, "is the PX or, as the Air Force calls it, the BX. They've got everything in there that you could possibly want to buy and a lot of stuff that makes no sense at all."

"Can we check it out?" asked one of the new guys.

"Later," said DeWeiss. "First, you all owe me a drink, and I want it at the Gunfighter's Club."

"What is this Gunfighter's Club?" asked Anderson.

"It's a club where anyone who is rated can go, but you have to have a set of wings to get in. You don't have wings, you don't go."

"Anyone with wings?"

"Anyone," said DeWeiss.

They passed through a gate, an air policeman guarding it. He was dressed in fatigues, wore a white helmet, and was armed with an M-16. He saluted the four of them as they walked by.

DeWeiss grinned and pointed at the ground. "No problem finding the club once you get into the general area."

There were giant green footprints painted on the street that led off to the south. In the distance, they could see a one-story building, the outside looking like any other, except for the sign that identified it.

"That's our destination."

They moved off, following footprints. The door was recessed, and a man sat outside it like the bouncer of an expensive bar, checking IDs. Or maybe he was like the guard of an Old West saloon. The only thing missing was the double-barreled shotgun to cradle in his lap. He stopped them and said, "No wings, you don't get in."

DeWeiss looked at his three companions and saw that none of them had any insignia sewn to their uniforms. He shook his head and said, "These guys are pilots."

"Can you prove that?"

DeWeiss shrugged, but Anderson said, "I've got my instrument ticket. Shows that I'm allowed to fly on instruments in bad weather, if the airfield is being overrun."

"Dig it out," said the man.

Anderson showed his instrument ticket.

"Okay, you can go in too."

The other two men followed suit, and the man nodded. "Wouldn't have this problem if you'd wear your wings. Shit, you'd think anyone authorized to wear wings would do it."

"They're FNGs. What do they know?"

The man nodded wisely and said, "Good point. Since they are FNGs, you'll be responsible for them."

"Right."

DeWeiss opened the door and Anderson entered. He stopped and moved out of the way. A series of lockboxes stood next to him. The club itself was visible down a short, narrow hallway and through another door. Rock music was vibrating the walls and rattling the glass in the door. Stage lights were flashing in time to the music.

DeWeiss followed the other two in and said, "Have to leave your weapons here if you've taken them with you. Lots of us refuse to leave them behind, but they don't want us gunning down each other."

With the weapons stored, they entered the club proper. It was a huge room with a bar on one side. Four men and two women worked behind it. Rows and rows of bottles lined the shelves in back of the bartenders. There was a huge mirror behind the shelves. In one corner was a raised stage where a girl danced in time to the music blaring from the various speakers. Tables and chairs were jammed everywhere, though those closest to the stage were filled with men in jungle fatigues and flight suits.

DeWeiss leaned close to Anderson and shouted, "Guys in gray are either Air Force or Navy. Guys in fatigues are probably Army."

"There ever any fights between the Army and everyone else?"

"Not as often as you'd think. Hell, man, we're all pilots." He grinned and then added, "Or, in the case of the Army and the Navy, we're all aviators." He pointed and ordered, "You boys find a seat, and I'll snag something to drink."

Anderson followed one of the other new guys as he pushed his way down toward the front. He flopped into a chair where he could watch the dancing girl as she shed her last bit of clothing. She twirled it around over her head as if it were a lariat, then threw it into the audience. One man leaped high and grabbed it.

Anderson dropped into one of the chairs and looked at the two new guys again. He couldn't remember their names, though they had been introduced in the club the night before. And then he remembered that one of them was Crawford. Charles Crawford.

"Hey, Crawford. Couldn't you have gotten any closer?"

Crawford leaned across the table and yelled, "No, this is close enough." He turned and stared at the woman's crotch.

DeWeiss arrived and set four beers on the table. He slipped into the empty chair, stared at the naked girl, and then picked up his beer.

"Should we be drinking?" asked Anderson.

"Beer isn't drinking," said DeWeiss. "You get out to some of the Special Forces camps, and they don't have water. You have to drink beer or go thirsty. Hell, a single beer isn't going to kill you."

Anderson turned and studied the club. There was air conditioning. The lighting was subdued and there was dark paneling on the walls. There were paintings of airplanes and helicopters in combat on the paneling. Overhead were the ever-present ceiling fans, spinning slowly and reminding Anderson of all the exotic locations in the Saturday-afternoon movies. Somehow Saigon did not spring to mind.

As he faced the door, it opened and a party burst in, shouting and laughing and demanding something to drink. The four men were wearing jungle fatigues that were wrinkled and sweat-stained, but the three women wore dresses that looked fresh.

DeWeiss turned then and announced, "Hey! I know those guys. Fly with the Long Trips. Live and work in Saigon. What a deal!" He stood up and waved. One of the men spotted him, waved, and then escorted the rest of the party over.

DeWeiss stood and said, "Hey, Frank, how's it going?"

Frank shot a glance at the women and said, "Not too bad at all. What are you doing here?"

"Teaching the fucking new guys about the war." He stood

and dragged another table closer. "Join us. We can't hang around too long anyway."

Frank pulled out a chair for one of the women and then sat down. He made introductions over the blaring rock music, but they were lost. Anderson was staring at the dark-haired woman. She was slender, with short, black hair and deep brown eyes. Her lips were thin, as was her nose. She glanced at Anderson, half smiled, and then turned away. He thought that Frank had said her name was Rachel, but he wasn't sure.

DeWeiss now ignored the FNGs, talking to the pilots from the Long Trips and trying to entertain the women. He sipped at his beer and glanced at his watch.

On the stage, the first woman had been replaced by another. She looked to be an American, tall and slim, with long hair and round eyes. For a moment she stood still, making eye contact with everyone in the audience, and then she began to move in time to the music. She smiled slyly, and glanced down as her fingers worked the buttons of the light blouse she wore. When she twirled, her short skirt swirled around her hips, showing the sheer panties she wore.

She danced to a slow song, stripping her blouse and dropping it to the stage. As the song ended, she rolled her skirt over her hips so that it pooled at her feet. When the pulsating beat of the next song started, she began to dance faster, a layer of sweat glistening on her body, highlighting it. She moved toward them, leaning toward Anderson, shaking herself at him. All he could think of was to grin at her.

DeWeiss slapped him on the shoulder and said, "Time to split."

Crawford stood and yelled, "But I'm in love."

"She'll keep. We've got to get back before Fox thinks I've stolen the aircraft and flown to safety in Cambodia. Which, by the way, isn't a bad idea."

They moved to the rear. Anderson stopped and took a final look at the woman dancing. She had taken off her panties and was now completely naked. She lifted a hand, waving at them as they left, and suddenly Anderson wanted to stay. He would buy her a drink and impress her with his stories of fighting the war to bring democracy to the peoples of Southeast Asia. And then he remembered that he had been in the country for about seventy-two hours and had no stories of fighting the war to bring democracy to the peoples of Southeast Asia.

Outside the club, he could hear again, though his ears still seemed to be vibrating. The air seemed to be more oppressive, hotter than it had been before. Sweat beaded and dripped and Anderson suddenly wanted to get out. He wanted to go home, because he didn't give a shit whether the South Vietnamese had democracy or not. In fact, he hadn't seen that many South Vietnamese, other than the first dancer.

DeWeiss stopped long enough to drop his pistol into his holster and said, "Anderson, you'll take the right seat on the way back. Little extra flight time for you. You think you can find your way back to Cu Chi?"

"I guess."

It wasn't sometime in the next couple of days that Anderson got his CA checkride, but much later, because of mission scheduling. Instead of getting the ride, he sat around the company area, only occasionally having something to do. Usually it was a make-work project designed to let Anderson, Crawford, and Morgan, the other fucking new guy, know that they were still in the Army. Brown sent Anderson to Saigon on the maintenance ship, to look into buying distinctive patches for the platoon from the vendors in Cholon. Anderson had no idea what he was doing, made a few half-hearted inquiries, and then flew back to Cu Chi with very little information.

One afternoon he helped sandbag a hootch, complaining that officers weren't supposed to do manual labor. Even the Geneva Convention said so. There was talk of filing a grievance, but when the work was done no one cared to go to Battalion to see the inspector general, because Fox came out and bought them all beers.

Most of the time Anderson had nothing to do except lay around reading the paperbacks that he bought at the PX. That was a twice-daily trek that ate up an hour or so. And when Fox mentioned to him and Crawford one afternoon that the club needed a jukebox, and that there was one sitting on a truck in the Twenty-fifth Infantry Division's area, they went off to steal it.

It turned out to be a simple thing to do. The truck was sitting by the side of the road, and there was no one around. They climbed in, Anderson behind the wheel, and drove off. In their own company area, they found three or four others to help unload the jukebox, and then took the truck back to where they had found it. They spent the afternoon filing the numbers off the jukebox, searching it carefully so that they got them all. They didn't want someone with a clipboard full of papers to come in and start matching numbers. That night, Fox complimented them on their ingenuity and their loyalty as the Beatles sang "Hey Jude."

Even that didn't help Anderson get into the air, because he still hadn't made his CA checkride. Each day he asked and each day he was told the same thing: "The instructor is busy, and he'll get you scheduled just as soon as possible."

Then, a few days later, Anderson was finally scheduled with the flight, but not really as a pilot. He would be in the cockpit, but he would be sandbagging again.

Anderson wasn't happy about sandbagging, which meant that no one trusted him to fly yet. He would just sit there, in the right seat, maybe change the radio frequencies if that had to be done, but not touch the controls. With only his basic checkride out of the way, he was the last pilot anyone wanted to fly with, but the situation demanded that he be scheduled.

Brown caught him on his way to the mess hall and said,

"Don't touch anything. Just keep your eyes open, try to learn what we're doing, and don't get in Engle's way."

"Yes, sir."

Brown took off his baseball cap, wiped the sweat from his face, and said, "Normally we wouldn't do this until you've had your checkride, but it can't be helped. Besides, you'll only be flying the spare."

"Yes, sir."

Anderson went in search of Engle, a tall, thin warrant officer Anderson had seen earlier, but who had not been pleased to learn that he would be flying with one of the fucking new guys. He'd said, "Let me tell you one thing. I'm short. I'm so short that I shouldn't be flying at night. When you're as short as I am, you don't fly at night, you don't fly in weather, and you never, but never, fuck with the red switches." He nearly collapsed at the humor of his own statement.

"All seriousness aside," he said, "you won't have to do anything. I don't want you to do anything. Just sit on your hands, don't ask stupid questions, and let me fly the aircraft. If we're lucky we won't be called out once we get to Tay Ninh. We can hang out in the club and fly home at midnight."

Anderson wanted to ask what the mission was, since he hadn't been told, other than that he was flying on the spare, but was afraid that was one of those stupid questions he had been warned not to ask.

"Your main job," continued Engle, "is to preflight the airplane. As soon as the aircraft assignments are posted, I want you to hotfoot it out there, check everything, and make the commo check. You understand?"

"Yes." Anderson understood totally. But if Engle was as short as he claimed, Anderson wondered why he would let a fucking new guy preflight.

Twenty minutes later Engle strolled into Anderson's room and asked, "What in the hell are you doing here?"

"Waiting for the mail. It just came into the mail room."

"You can get your mail when you get back. Aircraft assignments have been posted, and you're supposed to be out there preflighting, not screwing around in here."

"But the guy is in the next . . ."

"I don't give a shit. You're supposed to be on the flight line."

Anderson was going to say something about that, because Engle was only a warrant officer, but decided against it. It wasn't that important. Besides, he wasn't sure that there had been enough time for his letters to get home, and for everyone there to have had time to write back. At least that's what he told himself, because Susan hadn't written. He'd had two from his mother already.

He turned to the wall locker, opened it, and pulled out his helmet, pistol, and chicken plate. He checked the equipment slowly and then donned the chicken plate, giving the mail clerk a few extra minutes. It was the easiest way to handle it. Just as he thought he'd have to leave without his mail, the clerk looked in and said, "Got one for you, Mister Anderson."

Anderson reached out for the envelope, but before he could take it, Engle intercepted it. "You just get your ass out to the flight line."

Dropping his helmet on the floor, Anderson faced him. "I'll go when I get that letter."

"Don't mouth off to me, new guy. You do as you're told."

"Look, you don't outrank me here. When we get to the helicopter I might have to take that crap, but not here. Give me my letter."

Engle stared at him, focusing his eyes, trying to stare him down, but Anderson didn't fall for that. He returned the stare until Engle laughed and said, "Okay. But get your ass out to the airfield. We don't have much time."

Anderson took the letter and saw Susan's name on the return address. He wanted to rip it open and read it, but had made such a big deal out of getting it that he didn't want to antagonize Engle any further. He jammed it into the pocket on the front of his chicken plate, figuring that he could get the preflight done and then read it before takeoff. When he had seen Susan's name he had almost forgotten about Rachel and the dancer in the club. Almost, but not quite.

On the way to the airfield, he tried to figure out what her letter would say. There was a thrill of anticipation, a savoring of the knowledge that she had written, but also of the unknown—of not knowing what she had said. He could almost feel the heat of the letter, burning a hole in his pocket. It made the weight of the chicken plate vanish. It made the heat and humidity of South Vietnam vanish. It washed away the squalor of the company area, made the red dust that covered everything and got into everything vanish. All that was left was the single white envelope with Susan's name and return address on it.

He moved across the road, into the area where the helicopters were parked. Sandbagged revetments protected them from mortars and rockets. The walls were five feet tall, and many of the sandbags were ripped, spilling their sand. Each aircraft had its own revetment, and there were numbers painted on the front of each revetment. Anderson walked between two rows until he found the right aircraft. The crew chief and door gunner were already there, mounting the machine guns and checking the ammo.

Anderson tossed his helmet into the seat on the right side and then checked the book. If there was anything wrong, the pilots who had flown earlier would have written it up. He then began the preflight, opening the nose compartment to check the battery and the radios. He worked his way along the left side of the aircraft, checking the nav lights and the fuselage for damage and opening an access panel to examine the engine deck. He continued to the tail rotor. In flight school they had simply looked up at it, shaking the blades, but in Vietnam they climbed up on the stinger so that they could examine the tail-rotor linkage closely. Shaking the blades didn't tell you if the damn thing was about to fall off, while climbing up to look would. That done, he dropped to the ground and continued around, opening up an access hatch to look at the interior of the tail boom. That finished, he climbed up on the head to check the main rotor.

He was just about to jump down when Engle arrived and looked at him. "They moved up takeoff. We've got to hurry. You shouldn't have taken time to read that damn letter."

Anderson dropped to the ground, pulled the letter out of his pocket, and showed Engle that it wasn't open. "I planned on reading it when I finished."

"Should have read it when you had the chance." Engle grinned, having won the round.

Anderson climbed into the cockpit and strapped himself in. He touched the letter, but didn't take it out. Engle was in and had turned on the battery switch, starting the preflight check. Since the aircraft had been flown earlier in the day, they ignored the long checklist, opting for the one on the laminated card that was stuck in the map case at the end of the console.

When they finished, Engle put on his helmet, nodded for Anderson to do the same, and said, "Blackhawk operations, this is Blackhawk four two. Commo check."

"Roger four two. Commo check complete."

Engle sat back, looking at the other aircraft that had their engines running, their nav lights blinking. "Always turn on the rotating beacon before starting the engine. Let's everyone know what you're doing. You can read your letter now."

"That's all right, I'll wait." Anderson was showing off for Engle, trying to prove that he had willpower. And he was enjoying the anticipation so much that he didn't want to end it until he had to. He would wait.

The flight took off, one by one, maneuvering from the revetments to the edge of the runway, and then into the sky. As soon as one aircraft cleared the end of the runway, the next one would follow. Lead held at sixty knots, waiting for the formation to join, while the last two or three helicopters had to fly at ninety or a hundred knots to catch up.

As soon as the last aircraft had joined the formation there was a call on the radio, "Flight is joined in staggered trail."

"Roger. Lead's rolling over."

The nav lights on the helicopters were set on steady dim. That meant they were bright enough for the pilots to see them easily, but not so bright that people on the ground could find them. Engle pointed to the one bright, white light near the rotor mast that was invisible from the ground.

"We use that at night for formation flying. If you keep it over the center of the instrument panel, you'll be close to the right place in the formation."

Anderson watched the light on the aircraft to their left front, trying to memorize the angle in case Engle wanted him to fly. But Engle didn't seem inclined to relinquish his hold on the controls.

Over the intercom, Engle told him, "That little village down there is Trang Bang. You can see the road that leads into it. We'll stay south of that because of the gun target lines. Once we get to Go Dau Ha, we'll turn northwest to Tay Ninh."

Anderson nodded. Below he couldn't really see anything except a black ribbon that looked like a river, and a couple of dim lights. He didn't think that Trang Bang was much of a village, and if he had seen it in the daylight, he would have discovered that he was right.

They flew on in silence, Engle keeping control of the aircraft while giving Anderson a wealth of detail about the landmarks, the rivers, and the rules of flying in Vietnam. He called out landmarks and villages, but there was so little light and Anderson was so new to the country that he didn't remember much. Besides, there was the letter in his pocket, and that was destroying his concentration.

Fifty minutes after they had taken off, they were landing at Tay Ninh, cleared to land in the 115th Assault Helicopter Company's area for shutdown. They hovered between the revetments, landing there so that their aircraft had some protection. Once everyone had finished with a quick postflight, Engle said, "Follow me and learn."

They walked across a small road and through a gate that led to the 115th's living area. Engle pointed to the club and said, "You can wait in there. I'm going to visit friends. Don't leave the club and keep your ears open. If we get called out, they'll announce it on the company PA."

Anderson didn't say anything, he just headed for the club. It was a run-down building that looked as if a good wind would blow it over. Light leaked through holes in the walls, and there was noise coming from the inside. Once through the door, he found a bar with several stools in front. Six or seven tables were scattered around. There was a small room off to the right. The wooden floor was dirty. In one corner was an old black-and-white TV that had a picture in the center of the screen and broad black bands at the top and bottom.

Anderson worked his way to the bar, bought a Coke, and sat by himself at the one empty table. He pulled out his letter, slowly opened it, and got out the two sheets of paper. He looked at the signature, hoping for the best, but all it said was, "Peace, Susan."

He read the whole thing quickly, not understanding much of it. Then he went back through it, slowly, trying to figure out the meanings. There was nothing there to suggest that she loved him, or even liked him much. But she had written quickly, and he decided that he would write back, hoping she would respond just as quickly.

Once more he read the letter, and he began to realize that she had been afraid to commit much to paper because she wasn't sure how he felt. That seemed to be the problem. He felt his spirits lift. The only problem was that cryptic "Peace" at the end. He was afraid that she might not approve of the United States being involved in Vietnam, and that her disapproval would begin to extend to him.

Even sitting in a broken-down excuse of an officer's club

in Vietnam, Anderson wasn't sure how he felt. He thought that there was a mission to be accomplished. If people wanted to be free, then the United States should help, if the United States was asked to help. He didn't want to be there, but he felt an obligation to be. It was something that had to be done.

But Anderson didn't have any real political opinions about it. Except, he didn't believe that the United States would do something deceitful. Because of that, Anderson thought he should be where he was. Not that he wanted to be there, only that it was right that he be there. It was something that the people at home, the protesters, didn't seem to understand.

Of course, the self-justification might have come about because he'd gone with the flow. Rather than apply for college, he'd delayed until it was too late to get in, assuring himself a quick draft notice. Now that his laziness was catching up with him, he felt an obligation to believe that the United States was right to be in Vietnam. That was better than believing that his laziness had gotten him into something that he didn't understand at all.

Anderson turned his attention to the TV, trying to concentrate on the program. But his mind kept coming back to the letter and he would take it out and read it again. He would respond, quickly, he decided, and hope that Susan wouldn't become a protester who would stop writing to him. He didn't care if she was against the war, as long as she didn't turn against him. He would forget about Rachel and the dancer, because he didn't know them anyway.

Then, seeking more self-justification, he told himself that he was in Vietnam so that the Vietnamese people would have the right to protest if they wanted. To tell Americans that they couldn't protest, that they couldn't have opinions other than those supported by the government, defeated his whole purpose. Without the right to express unpopular opinions, or to believe what one wanted, there was no sense in fighting the war. Supposedly, that was the purpose.

He considered saying something about that to Susan in his next letter, and decided against it. He wouldn't suggest that there might be something wrong with having American troops in Vietnam, just in case the thought hadn't occurred to her. He would just tell her what was happening to him. He had decided to begin a letter, when the PA announced that all flight crews were to report to their aircraft.

Engle was already there. He was leaning against the nose of the helicopter, his arms folded. As Anderson approached, he said, "We're released. We go home now and put the aircraft to bed."

THREE

I T was still dark when someone shook him awake. He rolled to his back and stared up at the ceiling, trying to figure out what was happening.

"You Anderson?"

"Yeah."

"You're scheduled to fly." The man had turned and almost gotten through the door before Anderson stopped him.

"So what do I do now?" Anderson asked the retreating back.

The man stopped and glanced over his shoulder. "I'm just a clerk, sir. I don't know."

A voice came from the bottom bunk. "You get up, eat breakfast, and then go to operations to find out which aircraft you're assigned to. You go out, preflight, make commo check, and wait for the AC to arrive."

Anderson rolled to his stomach and looked down on the dark shape. "You flying this morning?"

"Of course. You can follow me, if you think it'll help."
The man swung his legs over the edge of the bed and rubbed
his face briskly. "Normally I skip breakfast and catch an
extra thirty minutes of sleep."

"Well, hey, Jason," said Anderson, "I don't want to put
you out."

"I'm awake now. Besides, I am sort of hungry."

Anderson sat up and then dropped to the floor as the man
turned on the light. Given the confusion of the flights and
the comings and goings of the pilots, Anderson had never
really talked to his roommate. They exchanged greetings,
but each had been going his own way, Anderson hanging
around with the other new guys, while Jason Timberlake and
the others avoided them as if they were diseased.

Anderson dressed quickly and then went into the front
room, but another man was standing at the sink, brushing his
teeth. Anderson dropped into the lawn chair and waited.
Timberlake came in and turned on the radio, which was
tuned to AFVN. Rock music started and, from the rear of
the hootch, someone shouted, "Turn that shit off while I'm
trying to sleep."

Anderson got his teeth brushed and then followed Timberlake to the mess hall. It was a huge structure, built in the
shape of an H. On one whole side, the enlisted men ate,
while on the other side the officers and NCOs ate. As they
entered, Timberlake and Anderson pointed to their names on
a huge board so that the clerk could check them off (because
the officers were paid separate rations and received money
for their meals not eaten).

They went through the line like that in a cafeteria, using
metal trays, forks, knives, and spoons. There were scrambled eggs, pancakes, bacon, sausage, and fried potatoes. At
the far end were bowls for dry cereal, but there was no fresh
milk, only powdered milk that when added to water turned
the water a dirty white.

They sat down at one of the tables set up for four. Timberlake took a cup to the tub at the front where there was

water and Kool-Aid. He brought some Kool-Aid back and then sat down. "Breakfast," he said, staring at the food. "No wonder I don't get up to eat it. This looks like shit."

"That's okay," said Anderson, putting his fork down. "It tastes like shit, too."

Timberlake stood. "You want coffee?"

"No, thanks."

Timberlake returned and sat down. He stared at the food and then pushed his plate away. "Nope, I'm sorry, I just can't do that to my body so early in the morning." He picked up a slice of toast and bit into it.

"So what's the drill," asked Anderson.

"You're sure a babe in the woods." Timberlake sipped his coffee and rocked back in his chair, hooking an arm over the rear of it. "Not really that much to it. The IP should be here to walk you through the first time, but once we finish breakfast, we head down to operations. They check us through and you pick up the survival radio. You also get the aircraft assignment and then go out to preflight. Crew chief should be out there and will have a flashlight for you. Once you've finished the preflight, you make commo check. That's all there is to it."

"What about the AC?"

Timberlake shrugged. "He comes strolling out about ten minutes before crank time. Everyone then checks in with lead and we then fly out to fight communism for the greater good of the free world, covering ourselves with glory in the process."

Anderson finished stuffing his face and pushed his tray away. "You know, it's funny. The airlines tell civilians not to eat a big meal before flying, to stay away from heavy foods, and that's exactly what they serve us here."

"You get airsick?"

"No. Just making a comment."

Timberlake pushed up the sleeve of his fatigue jacket so that he could check the time. "We'd better hotfoot it or we'll be late."

They picked up their trays and carried them to the window where the dirty dishes were stacked. They left them there and headed out of the mess hall. As they stepped outside, Anderson realized that it was somehow quieter. It was because they weren't near the roaring of the huge fans of the mess hall. It had actually been cool inside.

Back at the hootch, Timberlake put on his pistol. He had one of the Old West holsters that seemed popular. No one except the new guys wore the shoulder holsters issued to them.

"Where'd you get that?" asked Anderson.

"Gook shop by the PX. They make them."

When they had their equipment, they headed out, and walked around the headquarters hootch to the operations bunker. It was a massive thing, designed to take a rocket hit. They went down a short flight of steps set in a narrow passage lined with thick planks that oozed sap.

Timberlake tapped him on the shoulder and asked, "You ready?"

"Let's go."

Again, when they stepped out, Anderson realized that it was warmer, more muggy.

"Air conditioning," said Timberlake. "They tell us that the radios have to be kept out of the heat and humidity or they'll fall apart, but I think it's because the executive officer and the operations officer stay down there all the time. They have to be kept out of the heat and the humidity or they fall apart."

They crossed the road and walked out among the aircraft. As they approached the Huey Anderson was to fly, he asked, "What's it like?"

"What's what like?"

"This CA checkride."

Timberlake laughed. "Hell, it's simple. You sit on your side of the aircraft and prove that you can actually fly the thing. If you know how to hover, can stay close to the flight, and don't crash, you pass."

"It can't be that simple," said Anderson.

"Hell, man, you've got to get rid of that flight school mentality. You're now in the real world. Well, shit, Vietnam isn't the real world, but it's not flight school either. If you can fly, you pass. Don't sweat it."

"Right," said Anderson. It was the same story that he had been hearing since he entered flight school. The checkrides didn't really count, except that the men who busted them had cleaned their lockers and gone elsewhere. Rumor had it that they ended up in the infantry, walking through Vietnam.

Timberlake headed off into the darkness as Anderson tossed his gear into the right seat and turned to find the crew chief standing about two feet from him. The crew chief held out a flashlight and said, "I'd like it back."

"No problem." Anderson ran through the preflight, watching the bobbing lights on other aircraft. The door gunner was attaching the M-60s to the pussy mounts.

Anderson finished the preflight and noticed that a couple of the other aircraft had cranked. He sat there, staring through the Plexiglas, watching the sky to the east brighten. The lights on a couple of the other helicopters began to flash. Worried that he had forgotten something, he turned on the battery switch and came up on the company frequency.

"Chock three, commo check," he heard someone say.

"Roger three."

Anderson keyed his own mike and said, "Chock seven, commo check."

"Roger seven."

He sat back and listened as two more aircraft made their commo checks. No one else seemed to be interested in cranking, so he shut off the radios and the battery to wait. There was still a feeling that he had forgotten something, but he didn't know what it could be.

As he was about to make a radio call, to ask if he should crank, the door opposite him opened and the IP climbed in.

"Morning, Anderson," he said. "Let's get this son of a bitch fired up."

"We going through the whole checklist?"

"Fuck no. Besides, all that tells you is to make sure that everything is turned off and then to make sure that it's all turned on." DeWeiss ran a hand over the board above his head, then down the radio console, and glanced at the instrument panel. He checked all the circuit breakers and said, "Let's go."

Anderson made sure that the start generator was on, the main fuel was on, and then looked at DeWeiss, wondering if this was some kind of IP trick. Make the new guy look bad.

"Checklist?" asked Anderson.

DeWeiss grinned and pulled the laminated card from the map case. He began reading through the abbreviated checklist on the card.

Anderson followed the list, calling off the checks. Finally he rolled on the throttle, set it just below the flight idle detent, and glanced at the main rotor. It had been untied. Anderson looked out his window and shouted, "Clear!"

DeWeiss did the same, and the crew chief yelled, "Clear back here."

Anderson pulled the trigger and watched the gas producer as the needle climbed. He glanced at the exhaust-gas temperature gauge and saw that it was in the high green, but as the engine came up to speed, it dropped off.

Once they had the engine cranked, DeWeiss called operations and told them that the aircraft was up. Lead rogered the call.

There wasn't a lot that DeWeiss could explain while sitting on the ground. In flight school, everyone had been introduced to formation flying and, since the last four weeks had been a transition into the Huey, there was nothing new about it. Anderson sat in the right seat, the one that had been designed for the aircraft commander, and watched the instruments and listened to the radio calls.

"I'll take the first lift," said DeWeiss. "You'll take the second. You have questions, you ask them. That's what I'm here for."

Anderson nodded. He noticed that one of the helicopters was hovering, backing up out of its revetment. It hovered down the rows and stopped on the grass at the edge of the runway.

"Okay," said DeWeiss. "Before takeoff, we line up outside the revetments. That lets lead make one radio call to the tower for clearance and lets the flight join faster after takeoff."

They hovered from their revetment, the early-morning dew holding down the dust. They landed at the rear of the formation and a moment later heard, "Lead, you're ready with ten."

"Lead's on the go."

The first aircraft lifted off, climbing out toward the south. DeWeiss waited as the helicopters in front of him lifted and then took off when it was his turn. The Huey roared down the runway, gaining speed, and then DeWeiss hauled back on the cyclic to begin the climb out.

"These D models are underpowered. You have to be careful or you'll overstress the engine. You have to keep your eye on the torque meter so that you don't tear the engine apart."

Anderson glanced at the instrument and saw that they were pulling about forty pounds, well under the top. He then glanced out of the helicopter, at the base at Cu Chi. There were quite a few wooden buildings, each with a bright, shiny tin roof. The whole camp had an oval shape to it, and there was a road just inside the perimeter giving access to the entire bunker line. On the south side was a long line of Vietnamese waiting for the MPs to open the gate and let them in to begin their daily work. Anderson had heard that it was an agreement between the Vietnamese government and the American government. The United States was allowed to have the big camp on Vietnamese soil as long as they employed a large number of Vietnamese.

"This road we're crossing is Highway One," said DeWeiss over the intercom. "It leads to Saigon and into Cambodia."

Anderson looked down and saw a two-lane highway. He was sure that it was the same one that DeWeiss had pointed out during the earlier checkride.

"Now we're heading to Fire Support Base Patton, which is north of the road, but we have to stay south until we're beyond Trang Bang. The problem is the artillery. Before takeoff, you've got to call Cu Chi arty and give them your location and your destination. They'll tell you if anything is shooting and how to avoid flying through the gun target lines, which is one of the quickest ways to get killed. We fly south of Highway One to Trang Bang and then turn north, we'll be clear."

Again Anderson nodded, but wasn't sure what he had heard. This was something that no one had told him about in flight school.

"Frequencies for the various arty advisories are in the SOI. You spot the enemy, you can use the arty advisory to call in artillery."

DeWeiss slipped into his position in the formation, maintaining a one-to-two-rotor distance from the nearest aircraft.

"We fly a little tighter than they did in the World War. Provides better unit integrity when we hit a hot LZ. Notice the cross tubes on the skids? See the angle they form. That's the way you keep your position in the flight."

They turned north again. The ground below was covered with a scraggly-looking forest, not the thick, triple-canopy jungle that Anderson had heard about in flight school. He could see the ground, see abandoned enemy bunkers and the results of artillery that had been dropped on the area.

"We're now over the Ho Bo Woods," said DeWeiss. "We fly far enough north and you'll see the Saigon River, or the Song Sai Gon."

Then off in the distance appeared the circular pattern of a fire-support base. The Hueys headed toward it, descending slowly as they approached one side of it.

"These fire-support bases are built all over the place.

We'll pick up a company, take it out so that they can patrol, and bring them back at the end of the day."

On one side of the camp a cloud of red began to billow, and the flight turned toward it. On the intercom, DeWeiss said, "Lead made radio contact and they threw smoke. We count the loads and land next to ours."

Anderson didn't understand, but then saw groups of men standing in the grass just outside the wire of the base. DeWeiss landed next to one of them and, as the skids touched the ground, the men climbed on. Anderson turned and looked into the cargo compartment. Four of the men sat on the troopseat, two sat so that their feet were hanging out, and one man sat in the center of the floor.

"We're loaded, sir," said the crew chief.

Over the radio came, "You're down with ten and loaded."

"Lead's on the go."

They took off and joined the flight, and then turned to the east. They didn't go far before they started to orbit.

"Arty prep will go in first and then we land."

Anderson nodded, but had no idea where the LZ was. DeWeiss had brought maps with him, but hadn't shown them to Anderson. He'd just stuffed them into the map case and then ignored them.

The flash of fire caught Anderson's attention. He saw the column of black and gray rise up out of the ground in the distance. As he watched, there was another explosion and another, the dirt and debris thrown up by the artillery rounds. He turned in the seat, glancing out the cargo-compartment door. More explosions. First flashes of orange yellow, and then climbing clouds of black dirt.

Over the radio he heard, "Last rounds on the way. Lead's turning, inbound."

"Get your hands close to the controls," said DeWeiss, "but don't touch them."

One of the gunships approached from the front, coming straight at the flight like a driver playing chicken. It turned suddenly, the nose coming up so that Anderson saw the underside of the aircraft. The gunship turned, dropping lower, leading the flight toward the touchdown point.

"Lead, you have full suppression on the LZ."

"Roger."

They continued on, getting lower, closer to the ground. Anderson kept his hands near the controls, trying not to touch them, but to be ready in case something happened to DeWeiss. He jumped when the door guns opened up and then again as the gunships on either side of the flight began to pump rockets or machine-gun fire into the trees.

The gunship leading them buzzed through the LZ, and two smoke grenades tumbled from the rear.

"Lead, your touchdown point is thirty yards in front of the smoke."

"Roger."

Anderson tried to watch everything that was happening around him. There were small explosions in the trees as the rockets from the gunships detonated—loud, flat bangs that overpowered the roar of the Huey's turbines and the pop of the rotorblades. There was a hammering as the M-60s in the rear of the aircraft opened fire. On the aircraft in front of him, the grunts climbed out onto the skids so that they could leap into the LZ as the helicopter approached the ground.

"Chock four's taking fire on the left."

"Roger four."

Anderson shot a glance to the left, but there was nothing to see except the trees and bushes and the thick grass that carpeted the LZ. He wondered if he had heard right. There wasn't any evidence of the artillery prep or the enemy.

"Chock eight is taking fire on the left." The voice of the pilot was calm.

"Roger eight."

Anderson wanted to grab the controls and get out. There was shooting all around him, but it wasn't like it had been in the movies. There was no place to run and no way to duck. He had to sit there, slouched in the armored seat, his hands inches from the controls. DeWeiss didn't seem bothered by the calls, and the door guns had fallen silent.

Anderson glanced to the right, where another helicopter sat. He could plainly see the pilot, who seemed unconcerned with the firing. What struck Anderson was what a good target he made. A perfect target. Anderson wanted to get out. He could feel his heart hammering and his breathing accelerating, but there was nothing he could do.

Again the gunships rolled in, firing with miniguns into the trees. They were trying to suppress the enemy fire, which meant forcing the enemy to duck. Anderson still saw no sign of the enemy and didn't know how the pilots had known they were being shot at.

The grunts started leaping into the grass and disappearing. One or two popped up, fired a quick burst, and then disappeared again. Anderson wished they could get the hell out of there.

"Lead, you're down with ten. Fire on the left."

"Lead's on the go."

Anderson couldn't believe how calm everyone sounded. The enemy was there, maybe not visible, but there, shooting at them. Trying to kill them. And these guys sat there making calm radio calls. Anderson wanted out, wanted to take off and get out.

The flight lifted after what seemed an eternity, charged the trees, and then popped up and out of the LZ. The door guns, which had been firing, then had stopped when the grunts leaped out, opened fire briefly. The steady hammering seemed to relax Anderson. Twenty M-60 machine guns would keep the enemy from shooting at them. Then they fell silent again.

"You're out with ten. Fire from the left."

"Anyone take any hits?"

"Chock eight took some in the tail boom. Instruments in the green."

"Roger."

Over the intercom came, "You've got it."

Anderson didn't react for a moment. His mind was on the ground, where the enemy had shot at him. He could almost feel the bullets slamming into his body. Nothing else occupied his mind, just how vulnerable he'd been. Unlike John Wayne, he couldn't shoot back. Hell, there'd been no one to shoot at, even if he had drawn his weapon.

DeWeiss said, "You've got it."

The words suddenly penetrated, and Anderson took the controls. "I've got it."

DeWeiss sat back and wiped his gloved hand over his face under the edge of his helmet. He flipped the sun visor out of the way. "Join the flight and take up our position."

Anderson pulled in some pitch and dropped the nose to pick up speed.

"You have any questions?"

Anderson shot a glance at DeWeiss, realized that he was tensing up again now that he was flying, and forced himself to relax. He forced the thoughts of the enemy gunners from his mind, telling himself that they had missed him.

Finally he keyed the mike and said, "Just one. How could anyone tell we were being shot at?"

"Well, you can feel the rounds hitting the aircraft, especially if you have the controls, but I could hear the AKs firing. There were three or four of them."

"You could hear them?"

"The AK-47, the weapon carried by the majority of the enemy soldiers, makes a distinctive sound when it's being fired. Much different than the M-60 or the M-16. Sure, I could hear it. Now move up a little in the formation."

Anderson tried to move forward, found that he was pulling in pitch to maintain his position, and glanced at the torque meter.

"You'll have to drop down and out and then rejoin. You have to stay a little higher than the aircraft in front of you or you get into the rotorwash and have to use too much power to stay where you are."

Anderson lowered the pitch, dropped down, and rolled

out to the left, climbing up and rejoining. He held his position for a while, fighting all the controls, bobbing up and down and moving in and out. He felt sweat blossom on his forehead and drip under his arms. The muscles of his hands began to cramp from the death grip he had on the cyclic and collective. His shoulders ached and his legs were trembling. He didn't look at anything but the aircraft in front of him, trying to maintain his position in the flight.

"You making a cross-check?" asked DeWeiss.

Anderson shot a glance at the instrument panel and saw that two of the instruments were now at zero. "We seem to have a problem," ventured Anderson.

DeWeiss reached up and shoved the circuit breakers back in. "No, we have no problem, but you have to cross-check the instruments besides flying the aircraft."

Anderson nodded, but didn't take his hands from the controls or look at DeWeiss. He was afraid that the momentary break in concentration would cause him to fly into the helicopter in front of them. He remembered the seeming ease with which DeWeiss had guided the aircraft in the formation, his fingers barely holding the cyclic and his hand resting on top of the collective. He had adjusted the radios, checked the map, and pointed out a dozen landmarks. He had landed in an LZ under fire and hadn't seemed bothered by any of that. Now Anderson had control, and was afraid to breathe.

After what seemed hours, they landed again in the PZ where they had picked up the first group of soldiers. Anderson fought the helicopter all the way down, trying to stay with the formation.

"Count the damn loads," DeWeiss snapped. "Count the loads."

Anderson understood immediately and hovered forward, landing next to the seven grunts. As soon as the skids touched the ground, Anderson slammed the collective down, bouncing the aircraft. When they were safe, he relaxed for a moment, rolling his shoulders.

"Flight's down and loaded."

"Lead's on the go."

And Anderson's moment of relaxation was over. This wasn't like flight school, where there was time to get the mind going. It was bang, bang, bang, and the flight was on the go, taking off and climbing out. Anderson was unconsciously leaning forward in his seat, almost as if that would help him catch the flight. He had forgotten about the enemy soldiers who had shot at him, forgotten the fear of enemy bullets flying toward him, even though he could see nothing.

They joined up, but now it was harder to maintain his position. Now they had seven men, more than fifteen hundred extra pounds, on board. The controls were sluggish, the aircraft weak. It just wasn't like flying in flight school, where the helicopters were in top shape, the formations looser, and the density altitude did not conspire to weaken the aircraft even more. Heat and humidity affected the operation of the helicopters, just as it did the strength of the men.

"This time," said DeWeiss, "we probably won't take fire. There weren't that many guys shooting at us, and the grunts will have had a chance to sweep into the trees."

Anderson wanted to say "Good," but didn't trust himself with the intercom. He was too busy flying the aircraft.

As they approached the LZ, Anderson didn't have time to sightsee. He wasn't worried about anything other than maintaining his position and getting the aircraft on the ground safely. The fact that the enemy had shot at them on the first lift was again forgotten. Everything was forgotten except the cyclic and collective and the aircraft in front of him.

"Lead, you have negative suppression."

"Roger negative suppression."

And then they were on the ground and the grunts were leaping into the grass.

"You're down with ten, negative fire received."

"Lead's on the go."

They got out of the LZ, climbing to fifteen hundred feet quickly.

"Flight, that's it for now. You're released to stand by at Cu Chi."

"I've got it," said DeWeiss.

Anderson glanced to the left and said, "You've got it." He released the controls, relaxing. He felt drained, and he'd only been flying for thirty minutes. He closed his eyes for a moment and just let his muscles uncoil. As he did, he remembered that the VC had been there shooting at them. Suddenly that wasn't something to fear, but something to be proud of. The enemy had fired at him and missed. He was a warrior, tested by fire and combat, however light the fire and remote the combat.

"You remember the name of the highway out of Saigon?"

Anderson reached up with his hand and touched the back of it to his lips, suddenly overwhelmed with the mundane. They had been shot at by the enemy, but now it was time to return to learning the ropes. "Highway One."

"And the river north of the Ho Bo Woods?"

Anderson shrugged. He'd lost that one completely—too much thrown at him too fast, including the enemy bullets. There was much to remember about a country he hadn't even seen on a map until the newspapers started talking about the war in Vietnam. He remembered a teacher telling him how one day he'd never heard of Korea, and the next he was on a ship heading there. It was almost the same thing.

They landed at Cu Chi and shut down, leaving the helicopters parked near the runway rather than putting them into the revetments.

"Take your gear," said DeWeiss. "I'll be flying with Crawford on the next lift. You be in operations about three this afternoon."

Anderson didn't move. "How'd I do?"

"I'll debrief you and the others at the same time. That's why I want you all in operations this afternoon. Now, you fill out the book."

Anderson took the green, loose-leaf binder out of the map case and filled out the log, setting it up as cross-country flying rather than local. He signed it off and stuffed it back into the case. He grabbed his gear and then headed across the road to the company area.

Brown, the platoon leader, caught him and asked, "How'd it go?"

Anderson shrugged. "I'll find out this afternoon, when the flight gets back."

"Well, don't worry about it. You'd really have to fuck up not to pass."

FOUR

ANDERSON spent the rest of the morning and part of the afternoon in the operations bunker, studying the maps and reading the various regulations that governed the conduct of the war. He learned that the river to the north was the Song Sai Gon, just as he had been told, and learned that there was a similar river to the south called the Oriental. He found the Ho Bo Woods, War Zone C, War Zone D, and the Iron Triangle. He found that Trang Bang was not far from the town of Cu Chi, which was removed from the American base by a mile or so. There was a large swamp area to the south that eventually became the Plain of Reeds. To the west was the Parrot's Beak, which contained the Angel's Wing. There was Nui Ba Den, the Black Virgin Mountain, that could be seen in the distance and that located Tay Ninh for him. Close to that was the city where nearly a million Vietnamese lived.

Once he understood his area, he checked the intel map

kept by the operations officer. It showed the suspected locations of various enemy units, both Vietcong and North Vietnamese, drawn in red ink. It looked as if the map had been cut and had bled, there was so much red, but then no one seemed concerned about it.

The assistant operations officer, a tall, skinny warrant officer, was sitting in the rear of the bunker, moving papers around the beat-up and scarred metal desk. Behind him were more charts. Some of them were charts showing airways designated for Vietnam, others were aviation charts showing the local area, and the last was a map of Vietnam, showing the locations of all the major units in Vietnam. In a war movie, the last map would have been classified and covered. In Vietnam, everyone knew where everything was, so there was no reason to safeguard it.

Anderson stood in front of the desk for a moment and then said, "I've a couple of questions for you if you've got a minute."

The man dropped his pencil to the desk and laced his fingers behind his head. "I've always time to avoid this paperwork."

Anderson noticed that the man's name was Sadler. "Well, first, I want to know about these rules of engagement."

"What do you want to know?"

"Everything. That's something that was sprung on me today, and I didn't have any idea what they meant."

Sadler nodded and put his feet up on his desk. "Those in the know, wiser men than we, have declared that there shall be rules of engagement. They have studied war and realized that we, as Americans and guests of the Vietnamese, cannot be allowed to run wild. We must have guidance."

"The rules," said Anderson.

"Ah, yes, the rules. There is negative suppression, which means that we cannot shoot back unless we have spotted a specific target. If the enemy is clever, he can hose down the flight and not be fired upon. I'm sure that the civilian consultants in Washington, D.C., or elsewhere in the civilized world, where the firing is at a minimum, have a good reason for this particular rule."

"Uh-huh," said Anderson.

"Then there are normal rules. That means we can return fire for fire received, but are not allowed to shoot indiscriminately. Again Charlie and the other bad guys get to shoot first, but at least they've untied our hands."

"Providing that we've survived to shoot back," said Anderson.

"Exactly. And finally there is full suppression, which means we get to shoot first. Usually someone else flying under one of the first two variations of the rules of engagement has already been shot at, but that's why we're paid the big bucks."

Anderson rubbed his face and dropped into the chair that sat near the desk. He had suddenly realized he was the same rank as the assistant operations officer, so that he didn't have to wait to be asked to sit.

"You know, of course," said Sadler, "that the rules for the men flying in North Vietnam are even worse. There are pages and pages of restricted targets, places where they can't bomb, and targets they can't hit." Sadler dropped his feet to the floor and stood. He pointed to the map and said, "The Ho Chi Minh Trail comes out of North Vietnam, through Laos and Cambodia, and into South Vietnam. Because of various restrictions, the enemy can get some of his supplies through on the trail. We're not allowed to shut it down."

Anderson nodded, not knowing what to say. He'd read about that in the newspapers, but had never worried about it. Somehow it had become an abstract concept, argued by the senators and representatives in Washington and debated in various newspaper columns. But now it was becoming something personal, and he could hear the anger in Sadler's voice.

"The charade of American advisors has long been dropped. Hell, I'm not an advisor, you're not an advisor. We're flying combat missions daily, getting shot at, yet we're required to maintain the charade that Cambodia and Laos are neutral countries. Heaven forbid we do anything to violate the neutrality, because all the college assholes would be in the street protesting our widening the war. Shit."

Anderson was at a loss for words. All he had wanted to know was what the rules of engagement were.

"Sorry," said Sadler, "but I take it personally when people shoot at me and my so-called friends are at home waving the fucking North Vietnamese flag."

"I got shot at today," said Anderson.

"No, that wasn't shot at. I'm talking rounds through the windshield and the instrument panel disintegrating in front of you. I'm talking about bullets so thick in the LZ that you can't see how anyone survives." He waved a hand as if to wipe away what he had just said. "You'll wonder whose side the newspapers and the reporters are on. Christ, listen to me."

"All because I wanted the rules of engagement," said Anderson.

"Well, there's the problem. There shouldn't be rules of engagement. They shoot at us and we level their fucking village."

"Then you kill the innocent civilians," said Anderson.

"Providing there are innocent civilians. A case can be made that if they're shooting at you, they're not all that innocent." Again he held up his hand. "I know, the VC force them to shoot, force them to allow them to use the village as a headquarters, but we start fighting back and that shit will stop. You either fight the fucking war or you go home. We're just fucking around."

Anderson stood up and waited.

"Sorry about that. I'm getting short and I keep reading the newspaper. I won't do that anymore. Now, is there anything else that you wanted to know?"

"Not really. I just wanted to look at the maps and learn the rules of engagement."

Sadler pointed at the one that looked as if it had been

injured. "Don't worry about all that. They're just suspected locations of enemy troops some of the time. You could land out there and not find anyone. Hell, we don't know where they are and half the time they don't know where they are."

None of this was what Anderson wanted to hear. He didn't want to know that the American press was doing everything they could to help the enemy. He didn't want to hear about college students flying North Vietnamese flags or that no one seemed to know where the enemy was. He wanted to believe that he was participating in a great adventure that would make the world safe for democracy.

He glanced up at the clock and realized that the flight would be back soon. He left the operations end of the bunker and walked around to the counter where the scheduling board was located. The spec four behind it was reading from a paperback novel.

"Flight due in soon?"

"Got a final pickup before they're released. Probably thirty minutes to an hour before they return."

"Good," said Anderson. He ran up the stairs and out the door into the heat and humidity of the late afternoon.

Anderson, along with Crawford, was standing on the VIP pad across the road from the operations bunker when the flight returned. As the flight scattered, each pilot searching for the revetment in which to park his helicopter, one of them broke off, landing on the pad. As the Huey approached, Anderson turned his back, holding the soft, baseball-style cap on as the rotorwash ripped at everything loose and swirled it around in a miniature tornado.

As soon as the chopper was down, Anderson and Crawford hopped in the back. DeWeiss, sitting next to Morgan, turned and grinned at them and said, "We'll debrief the checkrides in a few minutes. Strap in because we're going for a ride."

With that, DeWeiss turned, and the aircraft picked up to a hover. They hesitated there for a moment and then took off, toward the north this time. They then turned to the south until they were south of Highway One. Then they turned east, descended, and low-leveled most of the way toward Saigon.

They landed at Hotel Three and shut down. DeWeiss dropped to the ground and said, "When you all pass your CA checkride, you get an evening at the Gunfighter's Club. We can eat dinner there and drink, as long as we're back in the company area by eight. Major Fox wants to announce your official joining of the flight at the officers' call tonight."

"That mean more Flaming Mimis?" asked Anderson.

"I'm afraid so."

"Terrific."

"One other thing that you men will want to know. It's a tradition that you buy my dinner and drinks. Hell, split three ways, that's hardly going to be a burden on anyone."

"Let's go," said Crawford.

They locked up the chopper as best they could and left Hotel Three, walking around the perimeter, through the gate, and out onto the base. They found the huge green footprints and followed them to the club. This time there was no trouble getting in, because everyone had wings sewn to his uniform. All those days down had given them the opportunity to have that done. When they entered, the Vietnamese dancer had just finished her routine, and the music died. The rumble of voices built, and Anderson saw the woman they had met the first time there. She was in civilian clothes, sitting with two other women.

"We ask them to join us?" he asked, pointing at them.

DeWeiss didn't answer. He walked straight to their table and said, "The Peter Pilots with me have just passed their checkrides, making them full-fledged members of the warrior class, and they would like you to join them. They said they're buying."

"Well, I don't know," said Rachel.

"Oh, and young Mister Anderson, the tall, thin one with

the brown hair, had his cherry broken this morning. Flight took some fire."

"Really?"

DeWeiss fell into the vacant chair and leaned close to her. "Bullets didn't come very close, but, hey, he was impressed with it."

"Then by all means we'll join you."

Crawford, Anderson, and Morgan grabbed chairs and dragged them over so that there was little free space around the table. DeWeiss introduced them all again, and then pointed to the woman. "You know Rachel. The blonde with the long hair is Sheila, and the blonde with the short hair is Debbie."

There were handshakes all around. For a moment, no one knew what to say, and then the music began and another dancer twirled onto the stage. She was the American that Crawford had thought he loved as they left the club the first time.

Anderson leaned across the table and asked Rachel, "What do you do here? In Saigon?"

"I work at the embassy as a secretary." She nodded at her friends. "We all do."

"Then you're not military," said Crawford, trying to stay in the conversation, although his attention was on the dancer.

"No," said Rachel. "I don't think there are any women here in the military, other than nurses."

"No," said Debbie, "I think there are a couple over at MACV headquarters, or at USARV. One or the other."

A waitress appeared, a small, Vietnamese woman with long black hair and dark, oval eyes. Even with the air conditioning, there was sweat on her forehead and staining her light blouse.

"You want?" she asked.

"We're going to have some dinner," said DeWeiss. "You ladies care to join us?"

"We've eaten, but you can buy us the promised drinks," said Debbie.

With that, the men ordered dinner, steaks and potatoes for each of them, along with a beer apiece. The women ordered mixed drinks. The waitress nodded as they spoke, but didn't write anything down.

"She'll get it wrong," said Morgan.

"Bet she doesn't," said Crawford.

"How much?"

"Five bucks says she'll get it right without any of us helping her."

"Done," said Morgan, reaching across the table to shake hands.

With that, Crawford turned his attention back to the dancer. He watched as she slowly stripped her way out of everything she wore. She kicked it around the stage and gyrated in time to the music. The others in the club stood and whistled and cheered and waved money at her, but she stayed away from them, dancing in time to the music, working up a good sweat.

When the music died, Crawford was on his feet. "I'll be right back."

He hurried toward the stage and intercepted the woman before she could disappear into the rear. She stood, her clothes held in her hands, breathing hard after the workout, staring at him, a smile on her lips.

"After you've dressed," said Crawford, "I'd like for you to join us. We'll buy you a drink."

"Dressed? You want me to get dressed first?"

Crawford was slightly confused by that. He looked at her and said, "Well, I thought you'd be more comfortable that way."

"Okay," she said, the smile spreading. "Where are you?"

Crawford turned and pointed. "Over there."

"Okay," she said again. "Be about ten minutes."

Crawford returned to the table and sat down as the food arrived. "She said that she'd join us."

After the waitress had given everyone their orders, she left, and Morgan sat there in awe. Just as Crawford had predicted, she'd gotten them all right. Silently, he handed over the money.

A few minutes later, the dancer joined them, pulling up a chair but sitting close to Crawford. He introduced himself and the others and then waited.

"I'm Linda," she said.

"You work in Saigon," said Crawford and then amended that. "I mean other than working here."

"Just here," she said. "I make good money for the amount of work I do."

The other women stared at her, as if she was something foreign. She stared back and then asked, "You got a problem?"

Rachel shrugged and said, "Hey, it's really none of our business how you earn a living."

"Damn straight," she said.

DeWeiss piped up, "We're celebrating a little bit tonight. These guys have become official warriors, and young Anderson there lost his cherry today."

Now Linda nodded in his direction and said, "Congratulations, or whatever."

"First combat assault and we take fire," he said proudly.

On impulse, Rachel leaned close and kissed him on the cheek. He turned toward her, surprised.

"A small reward for the warrior," she said.

"Well, thank you," said Anderson.

There was a burst of shouting from another corner of the club as half a dozen men grabbed a seventh and held him so that he was parallel to the ground. They stood so that they were in front of three tables lined up one against the other. There was a glass of beer on the far table. One of the men shouted, and they swung their victim back and forth, finally throwing him at the tables. He slid along their tops, on his belly, his hands outstretched so that he could snag the beer.

"Carrier landings," DeWeiss explained. "The Air Force

guys throw salt on the table and call them short-field land-ings."

"And what do helicopter pilots do?" asked Morgan.

"They just leap to the center of the table and yell hovering autorotation and sit there until someone hands them a beer. No wear and tear on the body."

"Sounds like a good plan to me," said Morgan.

It was then that one of the Air Force pilots, distinctive in his gray flight suit, stepped up behind Linda. He put his hands on her shoulders and announced, "It is time for her to sit with us."

Crawford stood up and said, "Shouldn't we ask the lady what she wants to do?"

"Nope. You've monopolized her long enough, and now she's going to join us." He hitchhiked a thumb over his shoulder, pointing at the two other Air Force pilots.

"Linda?" said Crawford.

"I guess I better go join them," she said.

"Remember, we've got them outnumbered and they're a bunch of college boys. You don't have to go if you don't want to."

"I'd rather stay here," she said.

"There you go," Crawford told the Air Force man. "She wants to stay."

The man moved so that he was closer to Crawford. He stuck his face down close so that his nose was only inches from Crawford's. "I say she goes."

Crawford glanced at DeWeiss and said, "I'm afraid that I don't know the protocol here."

Now the Air Force man spun and faced DeWeiss. "Daddy taking care of the little boys?"

DeWeiss grinned at the man and punched him in the face. He launched himself out of his chair, hit the man again, and then brought a knee up, flipping the man onto his back. Before anyone could react, DeWeiss was on the man, a handful of uniform bunched in his fist as he brought the man's head off the floor, but the Air Force pilot's eyes were closed.

His friends came forward and Crawford and Anderson leaped to meet them, but one held up his hand as if surrendering. "We don't want trouble. We'll just drag him home."

Crawford stepped back and said, "Be my guest. You should teach him some manners."

The man crouched and lifted, hauling the unconscious officer up off the floor. He swung him over his shoulder and said, "I think he's learned a few tonight."

As they disappeared, DeWeiss sat down at the table. He took a sip of beer and said, "The protocol is that you don't give the enemy the first punch and you don't take any shit off the Air Force. They think since the sky is blue, they own the world. Sometimes you have to remind them that they were once part of the Army, until we got tired of them and got rid of them."

They finished their dinner quickly, then. DeWeiss ordered another round of beers for the new guys, but ordered a Coke for himself. "We've got to fly back tonight yet," he reminded them.

"When will you be coming back?" Rachel asked, looking at Anderson.

He stared at her, taking it all in. He saw the beads of sweat at her hairline and on her upper lip. He watched a drop disappear down the front of her blouse and felt himself responding to her obvious interest. He wished there was a place they could go to be alone and talk. But that was impossible, because they had to get back to Cu Chi.

Rather than getting up, Anderson sat there, trying to think of a way to stay a few extra minutes. DeWeiss was up, drinking the last of his Coke.

"Come on, we've got to go."

Crawford looked at Linda and shrugged. "Guess that's it. I've got to go."

She took his hand and said, "Come on back sometime soon."

"You can count on it."

Anderson got to his feet then, his eyes still on Rachel. "I guess that's it." .

"Well, I'll be here tomorrow evening, if you care."

"Oh, I care," said Anderson, "I'm just not sure that I can do anything about it."

They flew back to the camp, arriving in time to top off the tanks in POL and then put the aircraft into its revetment. That done, they hurried to the company area, dropped off their flight gear, and then rushed to the club. The officers' call had not started, though most of the pilots were already there, drinking beers.

As they entered, Anderson was approached by Sadler, who leaned close and said, "When this is over, I want to talk to you about something important."

Anderson shrugged and said, "Sure."

With that Fox climbed onto the stage and waited for silence. He began the meeting by announcing that the fucking new guys had all passed the CA checkrides and would be thrown into the pool of Peter Pilots, lightening the load among them but offering no help for the aircraft commanders.

"While we're on that subject," said Fox, "I think it only fair that the Peter Pilots pay for the Flaming Mimis. Mr. Voorhes, if you'll pass a hat. Barkeep, the whiskey."

This time they hurried through the ritual and, although Anderson and Morgan failed to keep the fire burning, it was overlooked. The extra money was set up so that everyone could have free drinks for the rest of the evening.

That finished, Fox got serious. "First lift of the day took some fire. Infantry sweep into the trees revealed one body and one blood trail. They followed the trail and found the wounded VC, who died before medical treatment could be given."

There was a round of applause, and one of the gunship pilots yelled, "Who gets credit for the KIA?"

"Both belong to us. Infantry made light contact about thirty minutes later. They took two wounded but accounted for six more of the enemy. Rest of the day was a wash. No action, though one platoon did locate a small weapons cache. Four AKs, an SKS, and some ammo. Not much of anything important."

Fox rattled on, talking about what was scheduled for the next day and saying that flight assignments would be posted in the next thirty minutes in operations. With that, the meeting broke up.

As it did, Sadler pulled Anderson aside and asked, "You got a minute?"

"Sure."

Sadler glanced around to see if anyone was watching and then said, "After our talk this afternoon, I figured that we thought alike."

Anderson didn't remember much in the way of talking. He remembered a lecture that hadn't made much sense, but he said nothing.

"I'm putting together a deal, a . . . secret deal where we can get even with the enemy."

Anderson was still confused.

"What I want to do," said Sadler, "is file the serial numbers off fourteen pairs of rockets and hit one of the VC sanctuaries in Cambodia. Show them that we can hit them if we want and maybe force them to move deeper so that it is harder for them to get to South Vietnam."

"This legal?" asked Anderson.

"Fuck, no. Why do you think I'm filing the numbers off the rockets? So they can't be traced back to us. I figure we take a light fire team, low-level into Cambodia, make the hit, and low-level out. Maybe ten minutes over the target, maybe less."

Anderson didn't know what to say. He wasn't sure if Sadler was serious or if it was some kind of test. Maybe he should mention something to Captain Brown, or maybe to

Fox. Maybe he should keep his mouth shut. He just didn't know.

"You in or out?"

"I don't know."

"Well, you think about it, but don't go mentioning this around to a lot of people. This is a closed mission with a carefully chosen crew. We look at it as a way to get even, but we don't want a lot of people knowing about it."

"I won't say a word," said Anderson.

With that, Sadler spun and hurried from the club. Anderson realized that he never saw Sadler around the company area. The assistant ops officer must spend all his time in the ops bunker, rarely coming out.

Anderson walked to the bar and got himself a beer. He ignored the shouts of Crawford and Morgan, who were celebrating their success of the day. He dropped into a chair at a vacant table and tried to figure out whether Sadler was serious or just unbalanced. And then he wondered if he should go along. It would show everyone that he was one of the boys, ready to do anything that he could for the company.

Before he had a chance to figure it out, he was surrounded by people who demanded more Flaming Mimis in celebration. There was no way that he could refuse because, with Crawford and Morgan, he was the center of attention. Forgetting for the moment Sadler's plan, Anderson let himself be dragged to the bar for more of the ritual.

FIVE

I T was three days after the CA checkride that Anderson got his first opportunity to fly with the flight as a full-fledged Peter Pilot. Then it was almost a repeat of the checkride. Anderson was up before the sun, ate a small breakfast, and then headed to operations. Once he had the aircraft assignment, he went to the revetments and completed the preflight and the commo check. What he wanted to do then was lie down on the troopseat for a nap, but it was too close to takeoff.

The AC, a warrant officer named Romero, flew the first lift. He pointed out landmarks and told Anderson the frequencies of the various hospitals and aid stations. He kept up a running commentary, and then asked Anderson questions about what they had seen or what he had said. Coupled with the duties of flying the aircraft, it was like being in flight school again, though there would be no failing grades. If a mistake was made, it could cost several people their lives.

When they landed after hitting the refueling point, Romero flipped Anderson the SOI and said, "Study that. All the frequencies of all the units and airfields that we'll be using are in there. You don't have to memorize the damn thing, but you had better be familiar with it."

Anderson went to his hootch and found Timberlake lying on his bunk reading a paperback novel. Anderson sat down on the folding metal chair and said, "They give the pilots shit all the time?"

"Who do you mean?"

"I mean that Romero was on my ass the whole time asking questions and pointing out landmarks while I was trying to stay in formation. He never liked where I was either. Move it up, drop it back, you're too low."

Timberlake set his book down and said, "It gets easier. You got to remember that none of these guys wants to fly with you. You're the fucking new guy who doesn't know shit and is liable to make a mistake that kills them. They're going to make sure that you know how to get out of trouble and save their lives, if it comes to that."

Anderson had wanted someone to commiserate with, not a lecture on why things were the way they were. "Thanks a lot," he said.

"We've all gone through it. Once they know that you know, they'll ease up. No one wants to get killed because you fucked up."

"Least of all me," said Anderson.

"There you have it, then. Just pay attention and learn. It'll get easier, take my word for it."

"I can't wait."

Anderson flipped through the SOI, looking up units, call signs, and frequencies. When the company PA announced that all flight crews were to report to their aircraft, he hurried back out to the flight line.

The rest of the day was a repeat of the morning. They picked up soldiers in one location and moved them to another. Trail—the last helicopter in the flight—broke off a couple of times for special missions, and once the last three aircraft went. The flight shut down at a fire-support base for a while, and then returned to the company area. Late in the day, they picked up the soldiers and returned them to their camp.

When the flight returned, they landed at POL to top off the tanks and then headed for the revetments. Before they shut down, the crew chief poured a bucket of water into the filters in front of the rotor mast to clean them. That done, they shut down and Anderson filled out the book. Romero gave him the SOI and the survival radio, telling him to return them to operations.

As Anderson climbed out of the helicopter, Romero said, "By the way, you did all right today, for a new guy."

"Thanks," grumbled Anderson, not too pleased with the compliment.

The next two weeks worked much the same way. Anderson flew every two or three days and then had the rest of the time off. He spent some time in operations, studying the maps and the regulations, learning more about the AO and the rules they operated under. During that time, Sadler said nothing more to him about the secret mission to Cambodia.

Finally Anderson started to get scheduled every other day. The routine was always the same, but the days were not as physically draining as they had been. He was beginning to recognize the AO, and he had picked up some of the habits that made formation flying easier. The ACs relaxed with him, letting him fly for hours without asking a bunch of questions or pulling circuit breakers to see if he was paying attention on his cross-check. He began looking forward to the time in the air, rather than dreading it.

To make things better, they were making little contact with the enemy. Once or twice the flight took some fire, but no rounds struck any of the aircraft and it was all quickly suppressed. It was almost like flight school, the big worry being aircraft that were old and radios that didn't work.

Some of the time, while the flight crews were waiting to

be called out again, they played poker in the dayroom of one of the hootches. It was something to do while waiting, because each hand was quick and they rarely got caught in the middle of a game. When they did, highest hand took what was in the final pot before they ran out to fly.

Anderson sat there, watching the others, and when the last card was dealt to him, he picked up all his cards, irrationally fearing that it might be aces and eights, Wild Bill Hickok's famous last hand. It wasn't.

Timberlake flipped a scrip dime into the pot and said, "I'll open."

Crawford fanned his cards to peek at them. He studied them carefully, looked at the other players, back to his cards, and then at the dwindling pile of MPC—the monopoly money they were given instead of real cash—sitting in front of him. "I'm in."

All eyes turned to Anderson. He set his cards, face down, next to his revolver, which was sitting beside his money. Slowly he pushed a dime toward the pot.

"Christ, Andy, you act like that might be the last dime you'll ever see."

"The way the cards have been running, it could be."

Timberlake looked at DeWeiss. "You in or out? Come on. We haven't got all day."

"You got a big date, Timberlake? Just where the hell are you going?" snapped DeWeiss.

"Sorry," Timberlake said unnecesarily. "Would you please, if it suits you, either make a bet or get the hell out of the game?"

"Up a dime."

"Thank the Lord. Morgan?"

"What's that? Twenty cents to me?"

Now Timberlake was totally frustrated. He had wanted to play cards, and when he was playing cards, he concentrated only on that. "Yes. That's twenty cents to you. And if you raise the bet, then it will be thirty cents, and we'll all have to kick in some more money."

"Well, I'll call." Morgan put down his hand and, since he was the dealer, picked up the deck. "You want more cards?"

Timberlake took two. Anderson waited, tossed three away, and said, "I don't suppose I can have five?"

DeWeiss said, "I'll stick with these."

Timberlake shot him a glance. "Great. Caught from ambush."

"And the dealer takes three. Timberlake, it's up to you again."

Before he could speak, Captain Brown stepped into the doorway, looked at everyone, and said, "Anderson, what are you doing here?"

"Playing cards," he said, wondering if he had accidentally violated some unwritten rule. For a moment he thought that only aircraft commanders and senior Peter Pilots were allowed to play cards while the flight was on standby. He stared up at Brown.

"You were supposed to be at Battalion an hour ago." He stopped, stared at the five revolvers sitting on the table. "What in the hell are those weapons doing out?"

"Making sure that no one cheats," said Morgan. "You can't trust these guys as far as you can throw them."

"But you . . ." Brown let the thought die. He turned to Anderson. "You've got bunker duty tonight. You're to report to Captain Carson, at Battalion, as soon as possible."

"I'm flying today."

"What in the hell are you doing flying?"

"I was scheduled."

"No you weren't. You were supposed to be down because your name came up for bunker duty."

The sun had slipped so that it was directly behind Brown, shining in the door, silhouetting him. Anderson blinked at the light and put up a hand to shade his eyes. "Young was sick and they needed a pilot quickly. I was handy, so the operations officer told me to grab my gear."

"Well, it's too late to change that now." Brown looked at DeWeiss. "You'll have to grab one of those new guys to let him sandbag for you. Anderson, you'll have to get up to Battalion."

"Why not let one of the new guys have this. I flew all day."

"Because it's your turn, and the new guys aren't familiar enough with the area."

"But I don't know anything about being on bunker duty. I haven't been trained for that. I was trained to fly helicopters."

"Your words move me to tears, but they're expecting you at Battalion. Besides, there's nothing to it. The bunker NCO knows all about it. He does this every night. He'll take care of everything."

Anderson looked at his new cards, saw that he had drawn to an inside piece of shit, and threw them in. He picked up his pistol, snapped the cylinder closed, and put it in his holster—an Old West style holster that he'd gotten at the gook shop, just as Timberlake had said.

Brown said, "You can take the exec's jeep to get up to Battalion. It should be parked in front of the Orderly Room."

"What about my gear?"

"Somebody will get it and leave it in your room. Don't worry about that. Just get to Battalion."

"Okay. Where do I find Captain Carson?"

"Just get up there and ask. Christ, you're supposed to be an officer. Use your head."

Anderson had been to Battalion once, and he remembered little about it. He walked into the building, sandbagged in the same fashion as everything else in Vietnam, and entered a carpeted corridor. He came to a heavy oak door with Carson's name on it. He knocked once and heard a muffled voice telling him to come in.

Carson was sitting behind a huge wooden desk. There

were captured weapons hanging on the walls, bottoms of brass shells for ashtrays, and a framed document on the wall that turned out to be the basic award for the Air Medal.

When Anderson introduced himself, Carson tossed his pencil down and demanded, "Where in the hell have you been?"

"Flying."

"Flying?"

"Yes, sir." Anderson noticed that the man wasn't wearing wings.

"You were supposed to be here an hour ago," snapped Carson.

"I just found out."

"Well, that's your problem. Now, tonight, you'll be in charge of our section of the bunker line. You'll have to be in position by eighteen thirty tonight. After dark, no one is supposed to approach without the proper ID. The code for tonight is nineteen. You know what that means?"

"It's a challenge system. I give one number and the response has to be a number that makes a sum of nineteen."

Carson nodded, turned, and pointed to a map behind him. "These twelve bunkers are ours. The middle one, here, is the command bunker, and that's where you'll be. It has a land line back here, should have a sniperscope and radios. In addition, you'll take a PRC-25 out with you so that communication won't be interrupted."

He rattled through more instructions, but Anderson was finding it hard to concentrate on them. He was still angry about being given the job, because he had no training for it. There were five or six infantry lieutenants assigned to the company as Peter Pilots, and Anderson thought that they would be ideal for the job. Besides, the man here didn't seem to think that Anderson was going to do a very good job anyway.

Carson was pointing to different portions of the map, showing how things were to be defined. He turned from the map and said, "Your sergeant, who was here on time, has been briefed on all this. All you'll have to do is make a sitrep every hour or so. If nothing is happening, just report that there has been no activity."

Anderson was confused. "A cigarette report?"

"No, you idiot. A situation report. Sit rep. Didn't they teach you anything?"

Anderson went from confused back to angry. "They taught me how to fly helicopters, not sit around on the ground."

Carson broke in, his voice heavy with sarcasm. "We all have to do things that we don't like. There is a war on."

For a moment Anderson stared at the man—a captain who wasn't a pilot and who apparently spent the whole day in an air-conditioned office with nothing to do but wait for the bunker officer and NCO to show up. He didn't fly. Probably hadn't been shot at. Now he was telling Anderson that there was a war on. Inside the man's office, Anderson was hard-pressed to believe it, but he said nothing.

"If you have no more stupid questions, you're dismissed." Carson picked up his pencil and bent back to work.

Anderson stood watching him for a few seconds, some of his flight-school training so recent that he thought he should salute as he left, but Carson wouldn't look up. He turned and walked out.

Anderson had just enough time to draw an M-16 from supply, round up a steel pot, and find the jeep assigned to the bunker officer. Standing next to it was the sergeant of the guard.

When he saw Anderson, he climbed in behind the wheel and said, "We have to hurry, sir. We're late."

"I don't suppose there is a chance that I can get something to eat first."

"We're supposed to be there before dark so that I can show you the layout. After we get settled, I can probably get back here to find a sandwich or something."

Anderson climbed into the passenger side. "I don't understand this. There are six new guys here who haven't even got their checkrides out of the way, so they can't fly. One of them should be doing this."

The sergeant, who hadn't bothered to introduce himself, started the engine. "Yes, sir," he said noncommittally.

The aviation portion of the bunker line was on the northern side of the perimeter, facing an open area that extended for miles. Just outside the last strand of wire was a low-lying marshy area that would make attack difficult. There was a bridge over part of it, and one of the bunkers sat almost directly on the road that led to it. That bunker was armed with two M-60 machine guns and a .50-caliber. Near the center of the line was the command bunker, and next to it was an open space. Just before sunset, a tanklike vehicle drove up and plugged the hole.

For the first hour, Anderson walked up and down the line, trying to get an idea about the lay of the land. He found that most of the bunkers were a mess. Sandbags had burst open, spilling the dirt. The frameworks of some of the bunkers were broken, the splintered wood sticking up at all angles.

The inside was as bad as the outside. Equipment was stacked all over, and there didn't seem to be any logic to the system. There were no lights in the bunker, no flashlights, no lanterns. Anderson wondered how anyone was supposed to find anything. He moved to the firing slit and looked out. To the sergeant, he said, "Where are the firing controls for the claymores?"

The sergeant moved to the front of the bunker, sat down on an ammo case, and pawed through a stack of boxes, cans, and assorted equipment. "They're ... they're right here, sir."

Anderson tried to look at them, but it was getting too dark in the bunker. He took one of the controls and examined it. "Is it hooked up?"

"I don't think so. The ops officer is afraid that someone might fire them accidentally."

"How do you hook them up?"

"I don't really know, sir. No one ever asked before."

"Then what good are they?"

The sergeant shrugged. "We haven't had an alert for four months and hardly even get mortared. Why worry?"

Anderson stared at the slight man. Anderson knew almost nothing about the tactics of the situation. There were dim memories of a class or two taken in flight school that had told him some of the things he had to know. One of them was that the wires to the claymores should be hooked up and arranged in the firing order, so that, even in the dark, he could fire the one he wanted; and that they should be inspected every day. The way this system was arranged, he didn't even know if the mines were out there where they were supposed to be. Charlie could have sneaked up on some dark night and stolen the mines, or turned them around so that they would rake the bunkers instead of the attacking enemy.

Anderson opened the case that held the sniperscope. He lifted it out, turned it on, and surveyed the wire in front of him. In the distance, he could see something flashing in the little light left. He knew that there were cans fastened out there, with a rock in the bottom of each so that they would rattle if someone touched the concertina. But Anderson remembered, from the same class where he had learned about claymores, that VC sappers could move through the concertina quickly and easily, and that the Americans could hang all the cans on the wire they wanted, because the VC had learned how to move through it without disturbing it.

Outside, there was nothing to see. Anderson struggled to put the sniperscope back into the case. That done, he leaned on the sill of the firing port, and watched as the last of the light faded. Anderson finally turned away and said, "What about those sandwiches you were talking about?"

"I could go get them now if you want, sir."

"Any of the rest of you want a sandwich or a Coke?"

The sergeant went around and took up a collection, got

into the jeep, and disappeared down the road. Anderson crawled out of the bunker and stood behind part of the sandbag wall that connected the main bunker with the two tiny machine-gun bunkers on either side. For a few minutes he stood there, looking at the wire, and then turned so that he could watch the aircraft taking off and landing. He realized that he was being silhouetted by the landing lights and the runway lights, and ducked.

While they were waiting for the sergeant to return, one of the men stuck his head out of the door of the bunker and said, "Battalion operations called on the Lima Lima. They need a situation report."

Anderson turned on the radio, let it warm up, and made his first check-in. They asked why he had been late, and Anderson said, "Just finished inspecting the line and didn't want to make an incomplete report."

"Roger. Try to be on time. Ops out."

Anderson shut off the radio. He handed it back to one of the men in the bunker, but stayed outside. It was still early, not quite ten, so even if Charlie did hit them, it wouldn't be for another several hours. Anderson knew that Charlie attacked between two and three, when everything was at a low ebb, and the men were falling asleep. Everyone knew this, and yet, every time Charlie hit a base, he found people asleep all over the place.

Some of the enlisted men, who regularly volunteered for the duty because they had learned that it got them out of other details, had brought lawn chairs. They set them up behind the main bunker, propped their feet on the sandbags, and stared into the night. Anderson watched them for a couple of minutes.

Then a man loomed out of the dark, looked around, and said, to Anderson, "Sir, we have a problem with the land line from our bunker."

"Go on."

"We think that there has been a break in the line and need

to trace it, only the line is in front of the bunker. None of us want to screw around out there without telling everyone."

"You sure the line is in front of the bunker?"

"Yes, sir. We traced it there but didn't want to move out in front."

Anderson shook his head. He had spent hours telling everyone who would listen that he was unqualified to be the bunker officer because he didn't have the training, but he wasn't stupid enough to put a phone line in front of the bunker where Charlie could get at it. To the man he said, "That seems like a damn stupid place for it to be."

He just said, "Yes, sir."

Anderson said, "What do you want me to do about it?"

"I don't know, sir. We just thought that, maybe, we should try to get it fixed."

"All right." Anderson sat there for a minute, wondering what to do. Finally, he leaned in the bunker door and said, "One of you guys want to check the field-phone connections? See if the other bunkers will answer."

One of the men ran through the check and reported that everything was in good shape. Anderson nodded at the man, noted that the jeep wasn't back yet, and said, "Lead the way."

At the bunker, the staff sergeant who seemed to be in charge said, "We've checked it several times, sir. It's got to be the line."

"I guess we'll have to follow it, then. Who has the claymore controls?"

The staff sergeant said, "They're in the front of the bunker."

"I don't know about the rest of you," said Anderson, "but I'm not going anywhere until you get them deactivated."

That done, Anderson picked up the PRC-25 and called for the sergeant of the guard, who had returned to the command bunker. When he answered, Anderson said, "I don't want anyone on the line of fire, unless I pass the word. You understand, no one, and I mean no one, is to fire any weapon without checking with me."

"But, sir," protested the sergeant, "what if we are attacked? You can't order us not to shoot."

Anderson, feeling his first power ever as an Army officer said, "Yes I can. I'm going out in front and I don't want anyone shooting without my clearance. If they do, it's your ass. You got that?"

"Yes, sir."

Anderson could detect a note of sarcasm in the sergeant's voice, but he ignored it. He didn't care how the man felt about the order, just as long as he knew that no one on the line was going to be shooting at movement in front of the line.

Anderson signed off, and then surveyed the open field in front of the bunker. "I sure don't want to go out there with only this revolver." He had left the M-16 at the command bunker, figuring that he wouldn't need it.

"You're welcome to borrow this," said one of the guards, holding out his weapon.

Anderson took it. He stepped to the low, sandbag wall, and hesitated. To the sergeant, he said, "We'll go over one at a time." Anderson stood, hopped over the wall, and crouched, trying not to silhouette himself against the lights from the airfield, and scanned the open ground in front. The others joined him, and he told them to hold up for a moment so that he could be sure that there was no movement in the fields in front of them. When he was satisfied that they were alone, he asked where the common wire was.

One of the guards said, "Follow me."

They worked their way to the bunker and, near the base, one of the guards picked up the wire. He looked at Anderson, waiting for instructions.

"Okay, let's go. Everyone has been alerted about us."

He moved forward, letting the wire run through his hand, looking for the break. They hadn't gotten far when he found it. They were near the side of a sandbag wall. For some reason, no one had thought to bring any electrician's tape to repair the break. Anderson sent one of the men back for it, kicking himself for forgetting such a simple thing, and then telling himself that he was doing a hell of a job, since no one seemed interested in helping him.

A few minutes later there was movement from the direction of the bunkers, but Anderson was getting into his role of platoon leader and war hero. He whispered, "Eleven."

The movement stopped and a voice said, "Oh, shit. Ah, eight."

"Come ahead."

"Sorry. I almost forgot the code for tonight."

Ignoring that, Anderson said, "Can you repair the break?"

"Piece of cake."

From behind him someone whispered, "Sir, I think I can see something in the wire."

"Okay. No one make a sound." Anderson crouched down, setting the M-16 carefully beside him, trying to keep the barrel out of the dirt. Basic training had taught him that much. And it had taught him that a low profile would give him a better chance to see something if he could silhouette it against the sky.

In the distance, about the third or fourth strand out, he thought he could see something moving. It could be just a bush blowing in the breeze, except there wasn't much breeze. Anderson turned back, looking over his shoulder. "You guys about done?"

"All set."

"Then let's go back, carefully. Everyone stay low." It had suddenly dawned on Anderson that someone might have cut the line to set an ambush, and that he had walked right into it. Sweat popped out on his forehead and soaked his armpits. Slowly they fell back. It was only twenty or thirty feet to the bunker, but it looked to be miles.

Off to his right, Anderson caught another movement, as if someone had tried to flank them. He stopped long enough to scan the countryside. He suddenly knew that there was someone out there. He hadn't really seen anything. He just felt it in his bones. For a moment he believed that he was going to die because no one had taught him how to defend a bunker. He. had climbed out in front of the line the first chance he was given, and now wasn't sure that he could get himself back.

Just as he turned to begin crawling, he saw the movement again. They had reached the wall, but no one had been inclined to go over it yet. Anderson whispered to them, "I think I see someone out there. I'll shout the code. You guys wait a five count and if there is no response, go over the wall. I'll cover. Then you can cover me."

"Right."

"Okay, then. Here goes." Anderson put one hand next to his mouth, keeping the other on the pistol grip of the M-16. "Five."

Silently, Anderson counted to himself. "One. Two." He put his chin on the stock of the M-16 in the best tradition of night firing, trying to remember everything the sergeant in basic had told him. All he could remember was that he wasn't supposed to use the sights.

"Three. Four." Still no reply.

At "Five!" he shouted to the men, "Go," and pulled the trigger, hoping that the clown he had borrowed it from hadn't loaded it with tracers. It was on full automatic and he emptied it in the direction that he had seen the shapes.

When it quit firing and the bolt locked back, Anderson stood, drew his pistol, fired twice, and dived over the wall. Suddenly the whole bunker erupted. They had been waiting for him to clear the wall before they fired. There was a strange cracking, different from the M-16 and the M-60. Someone said, "AK-47."

The wall above them seemed to explode, showering them with dirt. Anderson hunched over, one hand on the OD baseball cap that he wore. "Christ," he said. He scrambled forward to the main bunker and grabbed the microphone of the

PRC-25, nearly screaming at the sergeant of the guard: "We're clear. If you see movement, you can open fire."

But even as he said that, the firing around him tapered off. There was no more incoming.

Anderson crawled to the main bunker and dropped down inside it. He breathed deeply several times, hoping that when he spoke, his voice wouldn't betray him. "You see anything out there?"

They were surveying the field with a starlight scope. "No, sir. Nothing moving out there now."

Anderson backed away from the firing port, toward the rear wall of the bunker. He could see the light-gray rectangle of the slit, but no detail. He didn't care, because he knew that he was out of his depth. No one during his short Army career had told him anything about this. He wasn't sure how much more he could take.

He was trying to figure out his next move, when one of the other guards stuck his head in and said, "Mister Anderson, I think someone at Battalion wants to talk to you on the radio."

Anderson took the mike and checked in. They asked him if he was shooting. "Roger. We took some incoming fire in return."

"You're to clear firing with us before you open up," the radio crackled back.

"Didn't seem prudent at the time."

"Three will be out there in a few minutes for a complete report."

Moments later Captain Carson roared up and slammed on the brakes so that he could slide to a stop in a cloud of dust.

Anderson waited until he was out of the jeep and then said, "Seven."

"Don't worry, it's only me."

It occurred to Anderson that he could now legally shoot the operations officer, but he repeated, "Seven."

Carson stopped, "Ah, a . . . eleven. No! Twelve."

"Advance."

When he was close, Carson hissed, "Now. What in the hell is going on out here?"

Anderson explained it quickly, thinking that they shouldn't be standing around outside the bunker talking about it. He finished by telling Carson that he thought there might be a body in the wire. One of the guards was watching to make sure that Charlie didn't try to sneak in to recover the body.

Carson listened to the story and then said, "So you went out there without clearing it."

"Seemed fairly routine at the time."

"We'll check to see if there was any movement out there. If we find no signs, you could be in big trouble," warned Carson.

He walked back to his jeep and called flight operations to request that a "firefly" make a low pass.

Minutes later, the aircraft, containing six landing lights in its cargo compartment that could be used to light up the ground, passed overhead. The bright light danced over the perimeter and pinpointed two bodies in black pajamas. That seemed to be that.

Carson pointed at Anderson and said, "Get in the jeep. We need to make a report at Battalion about this action."

"You think it's a good idea for me to leave the bunker line now?"

Carson stopped and turned to stare directly at Anderson. "What the hell is wrong with you? You show up late. You offer lame excuses about it. You waltz around in front of the bunkers without permission. Fire without permission. And now you question lawful orders. Yes it is a good idea, because I said it was. Now get in the jeep."

Anderson started to say something about the orders being questionable, but didn't want to get into any more trouble. He was trying to do his best, and every time he did something, it was wrong. He was angry now. So, without a word, he climbed into the jeep and waited for Carson to take them to Battalion.

For an hour, Anderson worked at filling out a wide variety of reports. They wanted everything from how many rounds had been fired to how many rounds had come in. They wanted to know the location of the fire, its direction, what time the first shot had been fired, how long the fight had lasted, and the number of enemy casualties. While he filled out the papers, he figured that someone with a computer would stuff all the information into it and then determine exactly what he had done wrong. It would make no difference that there had been no American casualties.

Finished, he took the stack of papers back into Carson, who took them without looking up and said, "Get back out to the line."

"I'll need a ride."

"Oh, shit. I don't have time for this. Find someone in the TOC to get you out there."

The rest of the night passed without incident. Anderson noticed that most of the guards started to fall asleep about four, but he didn't say anything. He knew that Charlie would have hit already if he had planned to. Charlie needed the darkness to cover his retreat, and it wasn't long to sunup. Besides, there were still people awake, watching.

A couple of hours later, three men arrived. They were the day guards. Since no one expected any trouble during the day, the force was cut to only three men, and only the main bunkers were manned.

Anderson called in, to report that they were securing the line. In the company area, he took a shower—it was cold, because the sun hadn't had time to heat the water in the giant tub over the shower room. Finally, he went to bed.

An hour later, someone was shaking him awake. Anderson realized that he could get sick of that. In fact, he was already sick of it.

The man said, "You're wanted at Battalion. They called and said that you had to get there immediately."

Anderson thought that it had to do with the firing on the line the night before. He envisioned having to report to the battalion commander, to explain the brief fight, and being awarded a medal for his part in the action, or offered a court-martial for screwing up. There was just no telling anymore. Anderson had lost his ability to tell what was the right way to do things. Or maybe he had never been told the Army way.

It proved to be nothing so dramatic. Carson was sitting in his air-conditioned office. He kept Anderson waiting until he finished his work and then said, "Do you remember, as I was briefing you last night, I said that you were responsible for the condition of the bunker line?"

"Yes."

"I have just come from there." He stopped, waited for Anderson to speak, and when he didn't said, "I have to tell you that I'm not pleased. There were cigarette butts scattered on the ground. I found Coke cans stacked in the bunkers, not thrown into the proper receptacles. In other words, the place was a mess. I want you to get the other members of the guard detail and I want you to go out there and police the area."

Anderson was stunned. Of all the ridiculous things he had heard during his two months in Vietnam, this had to be at the top of the list. He had flown the day before, been up all night on guard duty without the benefit of proper training or instruction, and now, rather than comment on any of that, he was told to go out and police the area. He knew that he wouldn't be able to ask the other guards to go out. It was too ridiculous. Too stupid. He would have to do it himself.

"Do you understand?" demanded Carson.

"Yes," said Anderson. He didn't call Carson sir. He couldn't bring himself to do that either.

"Yes, what?" Carson stared, waiting.

"Yes, it's clear."

"That's not what I meant."

"Then I guess it's not clear."

"What's not clear?" Carson screamed.

Anderson was shaking, but no longer with anger. He was trying to keep from laughing. He said, "How would I know if it's not clear?"

Carson exploded. "What the hell are you talking about? I want the bunker line cleaned. Immediately. Can you understand that?"

"Certainly." Anderson was still trying not to laugh. Maybe it was the lack of sleep, or the whole stupid situation, but he realized he just didn't care. He no longer cared enough to even be mad about it. It was just too stupid.

Back in the company area, after picking up a couple of cigarette butts and a Coke can, Anderson was stopped by Brown, who said, "Battalion operations officer called about you. Said he didn't appreciate your attitude. What happened?"

"I guess we just got off on the wrong foot. He was pissed because I was late, and couldn't understand even when I told him that I had been flying. Then there was that business on the bunker line and the firing. And finally, we hadn't policed the area well enough."

Brown shook his head. "You have to get along with these guys. They can make life miserable for you. Carson, fortunately, is about to go home, and he's not very well liked. But you have to watch your step."

"But, sir. I didn't do anything wrong. I was late because no one had told me. We returned fire for fire received—the normal rules of engagement."

"That's not the point and you know it. You've been in the Army long enough to know what the point is. You were damn lucky there were bodies in the wire."

Anderson stood unmoving. "Lucky there were bodies in the wire? What the hell does that mean? We're not supposed to shoot at the enemy?"

"I just meant that it confirmed that you took fire."

"And my word as an officer means nothing? It is only

important when it can be used against me, but not when it supports me?"

"Anderson, the whole point here is that you can't go antagonizing people you don't like, no matter what the circumstances. Let it go at that."

Anderson nodded and didn't speak. When Brown left, Anderson headed into his room. He climbed up on his bunk and went back to sleep, trying to forget everything that had happened the night before.

SIX

ANDERSON woke up covered in sweat. Bright light was seeping into the room from everywhere. He could hear a radio playing rock music in another hootch and he wondered what time it was. He swung his feet over the side of his bunk and dropped to the floor. His watch was lying in the bottom of his locker and he picked it up, squinting at the numbers. Just afternoon. He'd only been asleep for a couple of hours, but it felt like it had been all night.

He pulled on his fatigue pants and stumbled out of his room. He tried the sink, but the water hadn't been replaced in the barrel outside, so there was none. He wiped an arm over his forehead and found it covered with sweat. What he needed more than anything was a shower, but he knew that the officers' shower, if it had water, would be cold.

He returned to his room, grabbed a towel, clean underwear, and his shaving kit. He slipped his feet into shower shoes and headed for the enlisted men's shower. It was bigger and had a heater on the water supply. The water never got very hot, but it was better than the cold water available elsewhere.

Inside the shower, he stripped, hanging his pants and his towel on a hook and setting his shaving kit and clean underwear on a sink. He then showered, using the water to get wet and then turning it off. Unlike in the World, there wasn't an endless supply. Once he had washed himself, he rinsed and then stepped out to dry himself. With the towel then wrapped around his waist, he shaved and brushed his teeth.

Dressed in his clean underwear, and wearing only his fatigue pants, he returned to his hootch feeling much better. It was surprising that a shower had such powers. A quick shower and he was ready to fight the war again.

Instead, he put on a jungle jacket and wandered over to the club, where he could buy a cold Coke. He bought one and sat down at a wicker table near the floor fan that was trying to cool off the inside of the club. There was a magazine lying nearby, and Anderson picked it up, thumbing through it.

He was feeling good. The flying was no longer the hassle that it had been. He'd survived the night as the officer in charge of the bunker line. Somehow, standing out there with his steel pot and his pistols, he'd felt like John Wayne. Carson had been an asshole, but a lot of the regular Army officers were assholes. They were protecting careers and not worrying about fighting the war. So the man had gotten hot. It wouldn't hurt Anderson, because the man was outside his chain of command.

He sipped the Coke and stared out the open door, over the top of the magazine. *So this is Vietnam*, he thought. *This is fighting a war.* Certainly it was nothing like he had imagined it would be. So much free time, spent sitting around waiting to fly, or walking up to the PX to study the merchandise in case there was something that he wanted to buy. The enemy, distant shadows when seen, firing at the flight and missing most of the time. His closest approach to death had been the night before, and since he had been in charge, he had never thought about that. There was a job to be done and he was doing it.

Maybe that was the way with the Army. They trained you so well that when you ended up in action, the reactions were instinctive. Find a weapon and fire it. Use the radio and the technology to overwhelm the enemy. Training was the key. Teach a soldier what he needed to know and the average man became a soldier.

Sure, there would be cowards—men who wouldn't be able to overcome their fear no matter how good the training. But the majority of men would react just as they should. There would be no fleeing to the rear, as the young man had in Stephen Crane's novel. No sudden fear would cause Anderson to run. There was just a job to do—a job that he had learned well.

Maybe that was the key to bravery—each man knowing his job and knowing what had to be done. Then they did it without a lot of other thoughts intruding. There were no complex discussions about fear and death, but discussions about flying the aircraft and how to improve that skill—discussions about what was done wrong and what needed to be done.

He sipped his Coke and told himself that he hadn't been in a real battle yet, with the lead flying thick and fast. A few random shots fired at the flight, or a couple of bursts of machine-gun fire did not make a battle.

But he wasn't worried, because he knew how he would react. He knew that he would do his job and not let panic overwhelm him and destroy him. He knew it as well as he knew his own name, and he believed it with the same intensity that he believed in the United States and its goals.

A shadow fell across his table, and he looked up to see the assistant maintenance officer standing next to the table. He was an older man, in his mid to late thirties, and he didn't fly with the flight. He flew the maintenance runs, finding the supplies and parts that would keep the company's aircraft in the air. He was the hairiest man Anderson had ever seen. Without a shirt, it looked as if he was covered with thick, dark fur. His name was Bahror, and he was on his second tour in Vietnam.

"You scheduled for anything?" asked Bahror.

"Nope, down for the day."

"I need someone to sandbag for me. Give you a ride into Saigon, let you hang around in the PX there, take in a film or whatever. I do all the work."

Anderson drained his Coke. "How could I refuse a deal like that? I'll get my gear."

"Check in with ops and I'll meet you on the VIP pad. I've got a helicopter sitting there waiting."

"Okay," said Anderson. He left the club and returned to his hootch for his flight gear. With that in hand, he went to ops, told the clerk that he was going out in the maintenance ship, and then headed up the stairs. Outside, he walked across the road and found Bahror waiting for him.

"You want the right seat or the left?"

"I'll take the right. I'm used to it." He stepped around and opened the door.

"Okay. I'll do all the flying, unless you want to take the controls. If not, sit back and relax, enjoy the scenery."

"Sounds good," said Anderson. "Too good."

Anderson sat back and watched the world around him as they flew toward Saigon. He noticed that there were thousands of aircraft around. Jets and cargo planes and a dozen variety of helicopters. Flights of two and three and ten. There were almost as many helicopters in the air as there were trucks and jeeps on the ground.

As they approached Saigon, they dropped down, low-leveled under the active runway, and then popped up to approach Hotel Three. They landed, hovered to the side, and shut down.

Bahror flipped off the shoulder harness and turned. "It'll

take me about two hours to get everything taken care of. Where you going to be?"

"I'll just go over to the Gunfighter's Club and have a Coke."

"All right," said Bahror. "Wait there and I'll come by when I've finished."

Anderson got out and shut the door on his side of the helicoptor. "Okay. See you in a couple of hours."

While Bahror went into the terminal, Anderson headed out, through the gates and over toward the Club. He entered it and looked around, but found only a couple of people in it so early in the day. There was no music and no dancer.

Anderson went to the bar, got his Coke, and walked over to take a table. For a moment he sat there quietly, wondering what he would do for two hours. If he'd been thinking, he would have brought a book in case there was no one around. He grinned at himself, realizing that by no one he meant Rachel. If she wasn't around, he'd have no one to talk to.

Behind the stage he saw a flash of light, like a door had been opened, and then Linda came toward him. She was dressed in fatigues with no insignia on them. As she approached, she waved at the bartender and then dropped into the chair opposite him.

"How's it going?"

Anderson shrugged. "Well, I guess. You early?"

"Not all that much. I've got to start dancing in about twenty minutes. You be here to watch and cheer?"

"Sure, if you want. You know where Rachel is?"

Linda rubbed a hand over her face and said, "She's at work. She'll probably be in about five or so."

"Uh-huh. She come in every night?"

Linda looked at the floor and then said, "She didn't used to."

"What's that supposed to mean?"

The bartender arrived with a beer and set it down. He turned his attention to Anderson, who shook his head. When he vanished, Linda said, "It means that she keeps coming in hoping that you'll show up."

Anderson felt his stomach flip over but tried to keep his face blank. He forced himself not to smile. "Well, here I am," he said, trying to sound casual.

"Unfortunately, she's at work." Linda sipped her beer and then asked, "You want me to tell her that you were here asking about her?"

"Christ, no."

"High-school games. We're in the middle of a war, and everyone is playing high-school games."

"Just let me handle it," said Anderson.

"Okay," said Linda, standing. She finished her beer and then headed for the stage.

Anderson watched her leave. A few minutes later, she returned, danced, and stripped. When she finished that, she gathered her clothes and vanished through the curtain in the rear. Anderson was going to ask her to rejoin him, but Bahror arrived. He waved at Anderson and they left together.

As soon as they arrived back in the company area, Brown pointed at Anderson, "Where in the hell have you been?"

"Sandbagging on the maintenance flight to Saigon."

"Well, shit, you weren't supposed to be flying. You were supposed to be resting."

"What's the big deal?" asked Anderson.

"The big deal," said Brown, "is that you're scheduled for tonight. We've a night mission. Briefing in the club in twenty minutes. Now, you're not supposed to leave the area without telling someone where you're going."

"Hey," said Anderson. "I checked out through operations. I told them what I was doing."

"Next time, you check out with me."

Anderson shrugged. "You weren't around and Bahror needed someone right away."

"Then next time, you don't go. I can't have you people

flying all over the countryside without knowing where you are. You have a job to do here."

"I wasn't flying all over the countryside."

"I don't want to hear any more about it. If you're going off somewhere and don't plan to be back for an hour or so, you be sure to let someone know where you're going. You got that?"

"Yes, sir," said Anderson.

"Then get over to the club for the meeting."

"Yes, sir."

After telling the bar girls that they would have to go somewhere else for a couple of hours, Major Fox had the first sergeant close the doors and lock them. Outside, at each entrance and near the wall on the side that had neither entrance nor window, there were armed guards who were to prevent the Vietnamese from getting too close to the building. Major Fox wanted to be sure that no one overheard the briefing, and was taking every precaution to ensure that he got his way.

Anderson was at the bar, trying to convince Lieutenant Boxer, the temporary club officer, that he should give him a Coke before the briefing. "After all," argued Anderson, "no one cares if I drink a Coke, and it's hot in here."

Boxer slammed one to the bar and growled, "Schaffer bought the bar when his orders came."

Anderson slipped away from the bar, dropped into a chair at the rear of the group, and waited for the show to start.

Fox stepped to the center of the tiny stage and waited until all the lights had been extinguished, except for two spots just above his head. He held up his hand, shading his eyes, and said, "This is going to be a little different. I might remind you that everything said in this room is considered secret. That means we don't discuss it outside of here, we don't take notes, and we certainly don't leave anything behind that the Vietnamese might find interesting."

That said, he turned to the left and gestured. A short man

wearing jungle fatigues that had been starched to within an inch of their lives, climbed to the stage. He was half a foot shorter than Fox, had thinning hair, and was wearing his .45 in a low-slung holster as if he expected Black Bart to challenge him at any minute. He carried a large briefcase, and he waited while Lieutenant Boxer struggled to set up an easel. When he had everything set, and had been introduced as Major Hogan, the battalion intelligence officer, he said, "Tonight, about zero one zero zero, we expect a company-sized unit of VC to enter La Khe to collect taxes and recruit men."

Hogan went on to say that the aviation company would land just after one in the morning, in an attempt to catch the VC in the act. Another aviation unit was assigned to put in a blocking force in case the VC wanted to run, and a third company would insert a third unit.

Anderson sat there, stunned. He had been in Vietnam long enough to know that this was a special mission. They didn't normally land at night, in the midst of a Vietcong company. He didn't like the sound of it and, from the grumbling around him, no one else did either.

"We don't expect them to run," said Hogan. "We think, given the circumstances here, they'll stand and fight."

For the next hour, he answered questions, but the information remained the same—a night mission into an area where the VC would be waiting.

When Hogan finished, Fox simply added, "Crew assignments will be posted in ops in thirty minutes. Takeoff at midnight, commo check fifteen minutes before that, and preflight to begin an hour earlier. Any questions?"

As Anderson had learned in flight school, that was merely a way of ending the briefing. There were no more questions to ask.

On the airfield, Anderson noticed that things had changed. The ACs had drawn M-16s, something they rarely did, and the supply officer hadn't complained about all the extra paperwork. On the aircraft, Anderson saw that both the crew chief and the gunner had pushed piles of ammunition under the troopseat. Instead of the two or three magazines they normally carried for their M-16s, both had several bandoliers. The crew chief, a buck sergeant Anderson hadn't met before, had even found an M-79 grenade launcher, which he had loaded with canister rounds. These guys were going to war.

Ten minutes later, DeWeiss walked up, tossed his gear into the back, and then held out an extra box of .38 ammunition for Anderson. Finally, holding up a large piece of cloth, he said, "This is called a blood chit. In nine different languages and a variety of dialects, it says that we are Americans and that the American government will pay one thousand dollars for our safe return."

Anderson picked up one of the blood chits, examined it, and said, "Say, I've got a question. What if we run into a group of illiterates who can't read our blood chits?"

"Then you fall back five yards and punt."

DeWeiss spread his map out in the cargo compartment and, using his flashlight with a red lens cover on it, pointed to several marked areas. "Okay, this is the village, La Khe. We'll make our initial pickup at Fire Support Base Lincoln, about here. Our LZ is here. Now pay close attention." He took out a grease pencil and circled a small town. "From where we'll be, it'll just be a matter of choice where to go if I get hit. Depending on the situation, I would suggest Dau Tieng for minor wounds and Cu Chi for the more serious stuff. You know the evac hospital freq?"

"Sixty-two decimal five."

"Right. Now, if we go down and have to escape and evade, work your way to the south of the LZ, away from the village. If you do that, you should stay behind our lines. Challenge code is twelve." DeWeiss looked around then, first at Anderson and then at the crew chief and gunner. "You guys got any questions?"

The gunner stared at the map as if there was something

extremely fascinating on it. Finally he asked, "Is it going to be rough?"

"I don't know," said DeWeiss. "We might just walk in and out with no sweat. But this isn't one of their normal hit-or-miss operations. Someone has thought this through, and I thought we should be prepared, just in case."

In the cockpit, before the run-up, DeWeiss switched the intercoms to the "private" setting so that he could talk to Anderson without the crew chief or the gunner listening. He said, "This thing could turn out to be a lot rougher than I let on. There are good possibilities that we'll take some heavy fire, and that we'll get the worst of it because we're trail."

"I've been shot at before," said Anderson.

DeWeiss shook his head and laughed—a single bark that held no mirth. "No, you haven't really been shot at. We took a little fire. A few rounds. If the enemy is there, this is going to get real hairy."

Anderson now didn't know what to say. He'd been in Vietnam long enough to know what to expect. At least he thought he had been. Now he was being told that it didn't count. Flight school had prepared him to fly missions, that is, to control the aircraft, but it didn't or couldn't teach him what it would be like in the field. They had put men on the edges of the LZs in Alabama and let them shoot blanks at the flight, but somehow that just hadn't been the same. Everyone knew that the men on the ground weren't really trying to kill them. Now, all of a sudden, it dawned on him that the men at the edges of the LZ would be trying to put as many bullet holes in his helicopter as possible. All that raced through his mind, causing him to break out in a cold sweat.

Everything about this mission was different. First, there had been the classified briefing, and then the pilots drawing extra weapons. The briefing from the map was something new too. DeWeiss wanted him to know everything that he could about where they would be and what they would be doing.

He wiped his hand over his face and then looked at the sweat staining his glove. All he said was, "Terrific."

"Tonight we're going to do things a little differently. First, as we go into the LZ, I want you on the controls with me. Don't sit there with your hands close, but physically touch them. Let me fly it, don't fight me, but be right there with me. If anything happens, you'll be in a better position to take over."

He stopped for a moment and then said, "As we start the approach into the LZ, turn off the rotating target and then the nav lights. A Spooky will be dropping flares, so there will be plenty of light."

DeWeiss switched the intercom back to the normal position, they made commo check, and then lined up on the runway for a formation takeoff. They flew in a heavy right, found the troops in the PZ were lined up that way, and landed in formation. DeWeiss explained that it gave them better cover with the door guns that way. And Charlie couldn't aim at the lead ship and rake the whole flight.

As they touched down, DeWeiss said, "Remember, we won't be using the lights in the LZ."

"We're loaded, sir," said the crew chief.

Anderson glanced over his shoulder, into the cargo compartment. The troops were Americans, but Anderson already knew they would be. He had learned quickly that the Vietnamese didn't go where Charlie lived.

DeWeiss keyed the mike. "Scott," he said to the crew chief, "I want you to tell these guys to unload fast and hit the ground. This could be a hot one, and the faster they're out and the faster we're off, the better off they'll be."

"They know, sir," Scott said quietly.

For nearly twenty minutes they sat in the PZ, the engines running, the rotors turning. Anderson felt trapped. He was strapped to a seat, surrounded by Plexiglas, waiting for an opportunity to get shot at. A lot of things could have run through his mind. Instead he was trying to figure out how he got into the messes he did. There was a reoccurring pain in his stomach that reminded him where he was. Without the twinges, he would have forgotten, at least momentarily. But the instant he started to relax, there would be another, and he would remember what was about to happen. The enemy was out there, just waiting for him.

Lead finally called to say, "Come up to full RPM. We're on the go."

As they climbed out, DeWeiss almost whispered over the intercom, "Dim the panel lights."

Anderson did that and then sat with his hands nearly on controls. They made one orbit, turned at the RP, and headed in, toward the LZ. DeWeiss said, suddenly, "You've got it."

Anderson responded automatically. "I've got it." Out of the corner of his eye, he saw DeWeiss tighten his seat belt and shoulder harness and then lock the inertia reel. When he finished, he said, "I've got it."

Anderson turned and stared. That one motion of De-Weiss's did more to frighten Anderson than anything else he'd seen. DeWeiss was preparing for the worst, and if he was doing that, how bad would it get? There was nothing Anderson could use to compare it against, because he had no idea.

The first flare burst and he jerked upright, grabbing at the controls. DeWeiss said quickly, "Hey, take it easy. That was one of ours."

Anderson nodded dumbly and waited.

"Kill the rotating target."

Anderson didn't move. DeWeiss said again, "Turn off the rotating beacon and kill the nav lights."

As Anderson reached up to comply, they started a rapid descent, faster than normal. He could see the open field spread out in front of him, the shadows dancing on it as the flares descended on their parachutes—a strangely lit field that shifted as the flares popped and fell. For a moment, Anderson thought that no one on the ground cared that they were coming.

"Chock three's taking fire on the right."

Then the whole side of the village seemed to erupt. There was a bright flash by one of the hootches, and the gunships rolled in. Their door guns opened up. The flames from their barrels stabbed out.

Anderson felt a dozen vibrations shake the aircraft, and realized suddenly that they were bullets striking the metal skin.

"Flight's taking heavy fire from the right."

"Chock five is going down."

"Roger five."

"We have no casualties."

The village seemed to have come alive, and everyone there seemed to have a weapon. Green tracers lanced out at the choppers, and red ones were fired in reply. More flares burst overhead. There was an explosion near the center of the flight.

"Flight's taking RPGs."

"Chock eight is going down."

"Lead's taking heavy fire."

"Chock seven is going down."

"Who's on fire?"

There was another explosion, this one bigger than an RPG's. Anderson felt the concussion slam into his aircraft and heard a rain of shrapnel against the windshield. There was a loud snap and part of the windshield disappeared.

"Oh, Jesus," he whispered to himself, the sound of his voice lost in the roar of the turbine and the rattling of dozens of machine guns.

Over the radio someone said, in a voice that was icy calm, "Two exploded."

"Lead, make a go around. I say again. Do not land."

"Lead is rolling over."

DeWeiss pushed the cyclic forward, dumping the nose and picking up speed. The skids bushed through the grass as they shot across the LZ without stopping. The grunts were firing out the doors in violation of orders.

"Give me a head count."

In order, the aircraft checked in. Chocks two, five, seven, and eight were missing. Chock four reported that his crew chief was wounded and that several of the grunts had been hit. He was heading to Cu Chi.

"We lost four in the LZ," said Anderson, his voice unnaturally high.

"I know. Hang loose."

"Lead, this is six. Make a turn and head back into the LZ. You will be landing short of the original touchdown spot."

DeWeiss keyed the mike, "Ah, six, this is trail. Do you want me to pick up the downed crews?"

"Roger."

They turned, as directed, and headed back in. Again the side of the village erupted, but this time the gunships dropped everything they had. As Anderson's chopper touched the ground, the grunts were out, crouching in the grass, firing as fast as they could.

"Chock six is going down."

"Lead's on the go."

DeWeiss and his crew hovered forward, then stopped, and the crew from chock six leaped into the LZ, sprinting toward them. Once they were on board, DeWeiss hovered forward again, searching for the wreckage of the other aircraft.

Off to the left, there was a flash as one of the downed helicopters burst into flame. DeWeiss had been hovering at fifty knots. He pulled up suddenly, dropped the pitch, and kicked the pedals, sliding to a stop near the downed aircraft. Three of the crewmen ran forward, but the rest were missing. One of the ACs leaned in the window, shouting at DeWeiss. He keyed the mike on the intercom so that he could hear easier; the AC was now yelling into DeWeiss's boom mike.

"We got wounded."

Both the crew chief and the gunner leaped out, as did the crew from chock six. At that moment, the VC realized that there was still one aircraft in the area. They opened fire with everything they had.

DeWeiss grabbed his M-16 off the back of his seat and poked it out his window, firing on full automatic. The gunships were still out there, trying to suppress the enemy fire. Tracers from the miniguns, looking like a red death ray, danced among the hootches. Explosions from the rockets, looking like showers of electrical sparks, leaped up.

Over the radio came, "Trail, where are you?"

DeWeiss used the foot switch. "Still trying to get the downed crews."

"Roger."

"We're taking heavy fire from the right."

Out of the field, in the strange flickering light from the flares and the fires, a shape rose. Anderson stared at it, surprised that there was someone on that side of the aircraft. The man moved with the jerky motion of the old movies, the strobe effect of the fires making it seem like a series of stills flashed on a screen. The man was carrying an oddly shaped weapon and wasn't wearing a steel pot.

In a moment of horror, Anderson realized that it couldn't be an American. He was on the wrong side of the aircraft and was carrying an AK-47, the short stock and the banana clip unmistakable, even in the poor, uneven light.

Anderson dropped the controls and tried to pull his pistol. He scratched at the snap. Finally, he cleared the holster, pointed through the windshield, and fired all six rounds, jerking at the trigger. The bullets punched through the Plexiglas of the windshield. The enemy soldier staggered and then collapsed into the grass.

"What the hell?" shouted DeWeiss, turning. He accidentally broadcast it.

"Trail, what the hell is happening down there?"

"My pilot just shot a VC trying to get at us."

"Roger, trail, get the hell out of there."

A moment later, Anderson heard something scrape the floor in the cargo compartment. He was struggling to reload his pistol, but couldn't get at the ammo in the loops of his holster. He spun around, three bullets in his weapon, but saw a door gunner he recognized. The man's arm was hanging uselessly at his side. The sleeve of his uniform was torn and wet with blood. The scraping was caused by the butt of his rifle, as he dragged it with him.

The other crewmen followed. One of them nodded and held up a thumb. DeWeiss grabbed the controls, which Anderson had forgotten about when he fired at the enemy soldier.

"I've got it."

Anderson hit the floor switch. "You've got it."

DeWeiss eased the cyclic forward, kicking the pedals back and forth as they began to slide. As they picked up forward speed, he eased in the collective until they were climbing out. He had to be careful because they were badly overloaded.

Anderson felt a tap on his shoulder, and one of the ACs yelled at him, "We got everyone who was still alive. We left the dead behind."

DeWeiss heard and nodded. He relayed the message to C and C. Anderson sat there, his pistol clutched in his right hand, one round in his left. He was suddenly numb, unable to complete the simple task of reloading.

Over the radio, C and C rogered the call.

At Cu Chi, they dropped off the wounded at the Twelfth Evac Hospital and then went on to the VIP pad to let the other crewmen off so that they could get down to operations. They flew on to POL, and Anderson looked at DeWeiss and said, "I've got to get out."

Before DeWeiss could respond, Anderson was out of the aircraft, running across the open ground. He stopped by the road and dropped to his knees, thinking that he was going to be sick. He knelt there waiting, but nothing happened. He wiped the cold sweat from his forehead and smeared it on the chicken plate. He felt cold, although it was still hot and humid, despite the sun having set hours before.

Anderson wondered what was happening to him. He had

just gunned down a fellow human, a man who had done nothing to him. Anderson had no doubt that the man would have shot him, given the chance. And then he realized that he wasn't even sure that it was a man. The VC were an equal-opportunity employer, so there was a chance that Anderson had just killed a woman. His stomach flipped over, and he thought that he was finally going to lose his dinner.

And then he realized that he wasn't going to be sick. It was only in the movies that a man was sick after killing an enemy. Anderson was happy. Not happy that he had killed, but happy because it wasn't him lying in the dirt. Happy that he was alive to feel these things.

He stood up, took a deep breath, and looked into the night sky. There seemed to be a million stars there, blazing at him, but he knew it was only the lack of light on the ground— there was nothing on the ground to wash out the starlight. He headed slowly toward the aircraft, feeling slightly foolish, and wondering if tomorrow he would feel sick.

As he strapped in, DeWeiss asked, quietly, "You okay?"

Anderson nodded, and felt with his foot for the floor button. "I'm fine. I just needed to walk for a minute."

"Okay, then, you've got it. I have to look at the damage."

Anderson put his hands on the controls and said, "I've got it." He was happy to see that his hands were no longer shaking.

Five minutes later, DeWeiss climbed back in and, after settling himself into the seat, said, "We have damage to the tail boom and rotors. I sometimes think they stuck the tail boom on so that Charlie would have something to shoot at. But we're flyable. More than a lot of them can say." He sounded pleased.

They finished refueling and rejoined the flight at the edge of the runway. They shut down, and DeWeiss walked over to lead. He came back and told them, "Chock four is out of it. He took hits through the engine, transmission, and fuel cells. Lucky to have made it back here. Lead said he's trying to scrape up enough aircraft to fill out the flight, but I don't think he's going to make it. We lost too many tonight and have too many in for maintenance."

Anderson crawled into the back of the Huey and sat on the troopseat, staring toward the operations bunker. He let his mind wander, sometimes thinking about the man in the dark field that he had shot, wondering if he had been young, drafted, married, scared, fanatical, communist, or just in the wrong place at the wrong time. Still, he didn't feel remorse. At that moment, all he felt was tired. And, for some reason, alone.

That had come out of left field. He had been wondering how the people at home would feel about killing someone, even though it had been in a war. He wondered what Susan would say. He hadn't heard from her in several weeks, and now was no longer sure that he cared.

And as he thought of that, he realized what the problem was. There was no one that he cared enough about to share his feelings with. He was sure that his mother would be upset if he was killed, but he didn't know if her emotion would be real or faked. Maybe she would be upset only because that was what everyone expected, not what she felt. Like his expectation of being sick because he had seen that in the movies a dozen times. He wished that there was some-one waiting who would want to hear all this when he was ready to talk about it, but there wasn't. So, he felt alone.

Before he could go much further with it, he saw the lead AC run out of operations, swinging his arm above his head, telling them to crank up. Anderson leaned over, tapped De-Weiss, and pointed.

"Shit," was all he said.

Once they were airborne, DeWeiss said, "This might be a piece of cake. The grunts have had a chance to move into position. Charlie might be too busy to worry about us."

"But you don't believe that," said Anderson.

"Oh, who knows. It sounds good and it might even be right."

In the PZ, they had shuffled the loads because the flight

was down to seven aircraft. The village was easy to spot from the air because of the fires burning. When they got close, more flares dropped. But this time, there was very little fire from the village. Each time someone tried to shoot at the flight, a hundred weapons opened up, silencing the threat. They slipped in and out with no trouble, and no casualties.

As they cleared the LZ, DeWeiss said, "Lead, you're out with all seven. Little fire received."

"Lead, this is six. Return to base and shut down. You can stand by in the hootches, but be ready."

Anderson glanced at the clock in the instrument panel and was stunned to see that it was only a little after three. So much had been crammed into so little time. He had been sure that it was almost sunrise. He realized that he no longer thought of war as something that happens in the movies and covers the participants in glory. It was something real and deadly and covered no one with anything, except maybe a burial shroud.

In the company area, Anderson found his hootch nearly deserted. Next door, in the tiny dayroom, he found the majority of the officers who had flown and survived the first mission. Most were sitting around an octagonal table that held the pieces of a jigsaw puzzle. Enough had been completed so that he could tell that it was a New England covered bridge. To one side was a white refrigerator with its door open, and a man bent over searching for something inside. The overhead fan was on, but didn't seem to be doing anything at all.

Anderson found a lawn chair in the corner and sat down. He thought that he was too keyed up to sleep, that so much had happened that he wouldn't be tired for days, and that even if he was, he still wouldn't sleep.

At the refrigerator, the man, Tim Wilson, found a beer, held it up, and said, "Anybody else?"

"Put it away, Tim. We might have to fly again."

"Bull. Fucking. Shit. We ain't flying anything anywhere anymore. We don't have the aircraft left. We don't have the people. Now, anyone want a fucking beer?"

DeWeiss held up a hand. "Yeah. I'll take one."

Wilson found another and handed it to DeWeiss as he moved to an empty chair. He took a deep drink, slammed the can to the table, causing the puzzle to jump, and said, "A fucking go-around. We're getting shot to shit, and six tells us to make a go-around. Hell, we were almost there. We should have landed. It was insane to make a go-around then."

"How do you know? Maybe we would have been all chopped up. Maybe it was the most brilliant move of the war," said DeWeiss.

"I say again. Bull. Fucking. Shit."

"Ease up, Wilson."

"Ease up. We could have all been killed because he told us to go around."

"But we weren't," said DeWeiss.

Before he could say anything more, the door opened and one of the gunship pilots entered. They usually didn't condescend to enter the slick-driver area, but Walter Jackson was the exception. He often talked to the slick pilots. He said, "Thought you guys would want to know that we won."

"What the fuck does that mean?" asked Wilson.

Jackson walked to the refrigerator and took out a beer. He popped the tab, and after drinking said, "I mean that we came out ahead. Charlie took more losses then we did. We won."

"That's a little esoteric, Walt."

"Sure it is. But look at it this way. Last night we lost a couple of people, but Charlie lost nearly two hundred. He can shoot holes in all the airplanes he wants because we can always get more of them, but it's impossible to replace people that way. Once they're dead, they're dead. Since we lost only a couple of people, we're way ahead. Charlie was the big loser."

"That doesn't do the men who were killed any good."

"You're missing the point, Tim. No. It doesn't do them any good, but at least they helped put us ahead. Look at it this way. I figure in the last several months I've killed nearly a hundred and fifty VC. At least, I've gotten the credit for it. Now, if Charlie kills me tomorrow, I'm still ahead. He can only kill me once, so there is no way that he can ever catch up. If we keep our ratio up like that, we're going to win the war. Easily."

Wilson finished his beer and tossed the empty can out the door. It hit the wooden walk, bounced, and fell to the ground. "I'm going to bed before Jackson tells me how dying will end the war tomorrow."

"I didn't say it would end the war. But it would make life around here a little better."

There was a bark of laughter, and DeWeiss said, "You walked into that one."

"And out of here."

DeWeiss finished his beer and set the can on the table. He looked at Anderson and said, "Tim's right. We probably should try to catch some sleep, in case they want us."

A moment later the loudspeaker announced, "Attention in the company area. All flight crews stand down. All flight crews stand down."

"That means we put the aircraft to bed. A couple of minutes in ops and we're asleep."

SEVEN

MAJOR Fox sat at the conference table in his air-conditioned office and looked at the drawn faces of his platoon leaders and executive officer. It had been a long, horrible night, and Fox still had telegrams to draft about men now missing in action. The first notification to families was always that the man was missing in action, just in case the body had been misidentified. With the number of casualties taken the night before, and with some of the bodies still in aircraft on the ground in the LZ, Fox was taking no chances. Families would learn that their sons, fathers, brothers, husbands were missing in action.

But that was something, along with the letters, that could be put off for a few hours. Now he had to find a way to rebuild his company. Too many had died and too many were wounded for them to fly again that day.

The operations officer knocked and entered. "We've aircraft coming from our sister unit at Tay Ninh and spares coming from the Dragons at Bien Hoa and the supply pool at Tan Son Nhut. We'll have to get some pilots down to Tan Son Nhut to pick up the aircraft."

Fox snapped his fingers and waved the man forward, taking the paper from his hands. He scanned it and said, "With combat damage to those still flyable, we're about six short."

"Maintenance officer said that some of that was really minor."

"How minor?" asked Fox.

The man shrugged. "There was one aircraft with seventy-two holes in it, but nothing vital was hit. Some sheet-metal work and it will be flyable again in a couple of hours. Two in similar condition with all other damaged aircraft ready to fly inside of ninety hours."

Fox nodded and said, "Okay. Keep me posted as to our operational status and let the battalion CO know where we stand."

"Yes, sir."

When the man was gone, Fox looked at the men with him. "You heard that. In about four days we'll have our aircraft back up to operational levels, especially if we delay a couple of routine inspections. Now, what about pilots, especially ACs?"

The executive officer consulted a paper and said, "I've talked to Battalion and we can arrange a couple of inside-the-unit transfers. Bring in men from Tay Ninh and Dau Tieng. Group headquarters said they could get us a couple of people on loan."

"Which doesn't solve the long-term problem. I don't have the aircraft commanders to fill the flight."

"Well, sir," said Brown, "we've a number of men with over two hundred hours in-country. We could use them. And Timberlake has already moved to the left seat."

"I don't like that. The standard is three hundred."

"Yes, sir, but these are usual circumstances. What we could do is make them Peter Pilots in Charge—not really ACs—and keep them in the center of the flight where they can't get into trouble. It'll be a good learning experience for them, and later, when things calm down, we can train them as ACs."

"Anyone got a better idea?"

"The loaners we're getting will take up some of the slack," said the XO.

"But for how long?" asked Fox. "Their home units get into trouble, and they'll be jerked back. We'll be left with a hole in the TO and E."

"At best, it's a stopgap measure."

"We promote from within, we don't have that problem," said Brown.

"Who you got?" asked Fox.

"I've only got Anderson. Fairly steady now. A little immature, but what the hell, he's only nineteen. Put him in chock three or four and then don't break the flight so that he has to take lead or trail, and it shouldn't be a problem."

"Okay," said Fox, "on your recommendation, we'll elevate Anderson to PPIC."

Brown grinned and rubbed his chin. "Well, I'm not convinced I like the way you phrased that."

"There a problem with Anderson, now that you've brought him up?"

"No, sir," said Brown slowly. "It's just that we're moving him up without benefit of the AC training."

"If you feel that way, you shouldn't have brought it up."

"I'm sure he'll be fine. I'll see if I can't get him an orientation ride in the left seat. Maybe have him fly with me down to Tan Son Nhut."

"If that'll make you feel better about it." Fox looked at the First Platoon leader. "You have anyone?"

"Yes, sir. Crawford is at about the same level as Anderson. He probably could be advanced."

"And Morgan?"

"I'd feel better if we delayed on him. He'll come around, but he's just not ready."

Fox turned to the XO. "What's that do for us?"

"With Anderson and Crawford, we can now put up ten aircraft and a spare." He glanced at Captain Wilde and added, "Guns in good shape?"

"We weren't hit badly last night."

"Okay," said Fox. "That does it. Let's get back to work."

"What about the memorial services for the men killed last night?" asked Brown.

"Shit. Forgot about that." Fox pointed at the XO. "Get with the battalion chaplain and get something arranged for about eighteen hundred tonight in the club."

"All the flight crews will want to attend. Officers and enlisted."

"That's right," said Fox. "Didn't think of that. Maybe it would be better to hold it on the flight line."

"I'll make the arrangements," said the XO.

"And I'll get with operations for an aircraft," said Brown. "I'll fly with Anderson down to Tan Son Nhut with a couple of pilots to pick up the aircraft."

"They'll be available on the Air America pad," said the XO. He smiled when he saw the looks on the faces of the others. "Hey, they have a pad big enough to park the aircraft. We're not taking anything from the CIA."

"That's too bad," said Fox. "Might make things more interesting around here."

No one said a word to that.

Brown found Anderson sitting in the dayroom end of his hootch with two of the other pilots. In the background, the radio was playing rock softly. Timberlake had a beer that he was holding in one hand but not drinking from. DeWeiss was slowly shaking his head from side to side as if he still didn't believe what had happened. It was like a waiting room after the doctor had told the family that there was no hope. The discussions that had been raging earlier had ended, and now the fatigue was setting in—an emotional exhaustion that kept them from thinking and reacting to the night before.

"Anderson, grab your gear," said Brown.

"Christ, what for?"

Brown was going to snap at the younger man and tell him because those were his orders, but knew it would be wrong. Instead he explained. "We're going to Saigon to pick up some aircraft."

Anderson rubbed his eye with his finger as if there was something caught in it. He blinked and said, "Christ, we're supposed to be down today."

"I know, but this is something that has to be done."

Anderson wanted to argue and tell Brown to find someone else, but there really wasn't anyone else. Without a word he stood and dragged himself to his room. His helmet was on the floor where he had dropped it. He stooped and picked it up and then grabbed his chicken plate. His pistol was still strapped around his waist.

Brown was waiting for him when he returned. "We'll check through operations and see what's flyable."

"Yeah," said Anderson, "I didn't know we had anything left that would fly."

"Maintenance ship, the spare, and a couple that were down for their hundred-hour inspections."

"Who's going to fly the aircraft back from Saigon?" asked DeWeiss.

"You can have one of them if you want."

"Okay."

Timberlake put his beer down and said, "I'll go too."

"Meet us on the VIP pad in about twenty minutes. If you can find any Peter Pilots sitting around, grab them."

Brown turned and left, Anderson following him. Anderson was surprised that it was so bright outside. Although he could sit in the dayroom and look out the door, he had expected it to be overcast and raining. After what had happened the night before, he expected darkness and rain, as if the sky should somehow reflect the mood of gloom that had descended. It was too bright, with only an occasional puffy cloud drifting on a light breeze. It seemed a day that should be filled with happiness—boys and girls sneaking out of class for picnics, kids playing ball in vacant lots, people heading for the beach. After what had happened, there should have been rain and thunder and darkness.

In operations, they checked out the SOI and survival radio as a matter of routine. On the scheduling board, the numbers of the aircraft destroyed the night before had black lines drawn through them, and the names of the pilots killed had been wiped from the board. Anderson stood there staring at that, feeling cold and sick. It was so easy to eliminate friends—a wet rag, and you could wipe a name from the schedule. A couple of minutes and a new name could be written in.

Anderson stared at the clerk, a young man, probably older than Anderson, who was reading a paperback novel. The radio was blaring music and Anderson wanted to shout at him, but knew that it would do no good. The man didn't really know those men killed. He had seen them and talked to them, but didn't know them. It was like the high-school kids killed in a car crash. A shock, but a tragedy only for those who knew them well. A tragedy only for the family.

As they turned to climb the stairs, Brown said, "You'll take the left seat."

"I haven't flown left seat."

"I know," said Brown. "That's why you're going to do it today. You've got two hours to get used to it."

"What about . . ."

"Circumstances dictate that we move you over. This is going to be your checkride."

"Christ," said Anderson.

They reached the boardwalk and turned toward the flight line. "Now don't go getting uptight on me," warned Brown. "Given everything that's happened, this is a formality for the time being. You won't get AC orders yet, just PPIC."

They walked across the airfield to the revetments for the aircraft. Without thinking, Anderson started for the right side, remembered, and opened the left door. He threw his helmet into the seat, and then crawled into the cargo compartment to look at the book.

"You go through the preflight and I'll watch. You miss something and I'll let you know."

Anderson nodded and leaned over, turning on the battery switch and checking a few of the gauges and the master caution panel. He flipped the switch off and leaped out, moving to the front so that he could check the nose compartment. Brown stood by and watched everything he did, not saying a word until they climbed up on top to look at the rotor mast.

"You know the tolerances of the bearings?"

Anderson glanced at Brown and said, "Not really. They're so fine that I couldn't tell if something was out of tolerance or not. I know if there is supposed to be a little play or no play, and I can look at the slippage marks."

Brown shrugged. "I guess that's good enough."

As they were climbing down, Timberlake and DeWeiss along with a couple of the new guys arrived carrying their flight gear.

"Thought you were going to meet us at the VIP pad," said Brown.

"We thought we'd save some time and walk over here."

"We're about ready to crank," said Brown.

When Anderson opened the left door to climb in, DeWeiss said, "What gives here?"

"Giving Anderson a short course on being a PPIC," said Brown.

"Shouldn't the ACs discuss it?"

"After last night, there aren't enough left to discuss anything. Besides, it's just a temporary move."

DeWeiss stood staring for a moment, and then got into the cargo compartment. He strapped in and didn't speak.

While Brown watched, Anderson ran through the start and run-up procedures. When he finished, Brown said, "I've got it. I'll take off and let you see how it feels over there, and then you can go ahead and fly it."

Anderson nodded and listened in as Brown called the tower for clearance to take off. Once they were airborne, Anderson used one of the nav radios to pick up AFVN, and turned on the rock and roll music. The nav-two switch on the radio console had to be up for the other crew members to hear the music.

Once they had cleared the traffic pattern, Brown said, "You've got it."

Anderson put his hands on the controls and said, "I've got it."

Brown took his hands off and then said, "You won't notice much difference now, but landing and flying in the formation, there is quite a bit. Takes a couple of hours to get used to the experience."

Anderson nodded but wasn't sure that he believed what Brown was telling him. Flying the helicopter was basically flying the helicopter, no matter what seat he sat in.

They went through the ritual of low-leveling under the active runway. As they approached the ground, Anderson suddenly felt that he was losing sight of everything around him. He slowed the descent and glanced out the side window, realizing that it was his perspective. The instrument panel was now to his left. Reference points that he was used to seeing out the right window were invisible. He had to pick them up out the left.

To compensate, he popped up, flying at thirty or forty feet. He nosed over, gaining speed, and, once under the runway, hauled back on the cyclic until he was at five hundred feet. He entered the traffic pattern for Tan Son Nhut, requesting clearance to land at the Air America pad.

As he started the approach, Brown sat up straighter, his hands near the controls. Using the floor button for the intercom, Brown said, "Told you it was different."

"I wouldn't have believed it," said Anderson.

They turned and shot toward the silver-looking hangar with a C-47 sitting out front. They touched down, bounced once, and then rocked back and forth inches above the pad as Anderson fought the wind and rotorwash. He worked the pedals rapidly and jockeyed the cyclic, trying to stabilize the hover. Finally, in frustration, he dropped the collective. They landed hard, but they were down.

Timberlake unbuckled his seat belt and slapped Anderson on the shoulder. When the pilot looked back, Timberlake shouted over the sound of the turbine, "Don't forget to log all seven or eight of those landings."

Brown used the intercom to say, "It'll take about an hour to complete the paperwork. Why don't you go ahead and shut it down?"

"Yes, sir."

When the aircraft was shut down and tied down, Anderson climbed out and joined the others on the tarmac. Brown looked at his watch and said, "Why don't you all head over to the Gunfighter's Club, grab a Coke, and plan to come back here in an hour."

"I don't know," said DeWeiss.

"I do," responded Brown. "Go relax for a few minutes and then come back here. We'll head off then."

"I'm not much in the mood," said Timberlake.

"Look, I know how you all feel, but it won't help to sit around. Hoist one in the memory of those who died. We'll have a memorial service tonight."

Anderson took a deep breath and said, "Sure. The Gunfighter's Club. Let's go."

Timberlake stood still for a moment and then nodded. "All right."

As Brown disappeared into the Air America hangar, DeWeiss moved to the side where a jeep stood unattended. DeWeiss climbed behind the wheel and said, "Come on."

"You can't steal that jeep," said Timberlake.

"The hell," said DeWeiss. "Besides, I'm just borrowing it for an hour. No one will give a shit."

Anderson climbed into the passenger's side and said, "Let's go."

DeWeiss started the engine and the others leaped into the

rear. He backed up, turned, and then gunned the engine. They drove along the runways, where jets were taking off and landing. They went through one gate and turned down another road until they were in front of the club. DeWeiss stopped and turned off the engine. He was out and on his way into the club.

Before they entered, the heavy beat of the music could be heard. Anderson stopped at the door, his hand on the bar to pull it open.

"You really want to do this?"

Timberlake shrugged. "It's better than standing around in the heat out here."

Anderson opened the door and entered. He didn't bother putting his pistol into the lockbox. He pulled open the door to enter the club proper and again stopped. One of the Vietnamese girls was dancing on the stage naked.

Anderson stared at her, at the glistening sheen of sweat on her body as she moved in time to the music. It seemed such a stark contrast to everything that had happened in the last twenty-four hours. And yet there was something positive in the act, and in the cheering group of men near the stage, urging her to do more, to display more of herself to them.

Anderson shook his head and realized just how important the sacrifice of the men in the field was. No one really cared except for a limited number of people. If Anderson went out and died the next day, there would still be men watching the girls dance while they drank beer.

Maybe that was the whole key to fighting a war. Live each day as if it were the last, because it might be. And, if you survived, drink a beer in honor of those who didn't.

It was a confusing jumble. On the one hand, it seemed gross that there could be people who didn't care about the deaths of their fellow soldiers, and, on the other, maybe they were living the way they did because they soon could be dead too.

"Okay," said Anderson. "I'm getting a Coke. How about the rest of you?"

"All the way around," said DeWeiss. He was standing near the wall, watching the woman perform.

When Anderson got to the table with the drinks, Timberlake looked at him and said, "You feel right about this?"

"I feel fine about it," said Anderson. He dropped into a chair and added, "Maybe it's like Walt said. We won, and we should celebrate that."

"I'm sure that the men who died are celebrating."

The last thing that Anderson wanted to do was get into a philosophical discussion on the subject, so he just said, "Maybe they are."

"Bullshit."

"No," said DeWeiss. "Andy might be right on that. Or he might be wrong. I do know that we can't let this get to us now. Later, back in the World, we have to let the people know what happened here, what it was actually like, but now, we have to go on. We almost have to pretend that it never happened."

"Somehow that doesn't seem right," said Timberlake.

"But it doesn't seem wrong, either," said Anderson. "It's just the way things are. So we'll go to the memorial service and then we'll go out and fly the next day."

"Think of it as a wake," said DeWeiss. "We're not celebrating the death of friends, we're celebrating the privilege of knowing them. Look at it this way. If you were killed, how would you like people to react."

Anderson pointed at the naked woman and then the bar. "I think I would like them to have a party with women and booze. Just have a hell of a party and drink themselves silly."

"Then that's what we'll do when we get back to the company area," said DeWeiss. That said, he turned to watch the woman. "This is what we're fighting for," he said.

They watched the dancers, sipping Coke until it was time to head back to the Air America pad. They got up to leave, Timberlake pushing on ahead. As they hurried out the door, Anderson grabbed DeWeiss by the arm.

"Got a question for you."

"What's that?"

"You ever talk to Sadler about a special mission that he's got going?"

"Christ, Andy, he pull that one on you? He's been going to do it for six months. File the serial numbers off the rockets and attack the Vietcong in Cambodia."

"Then it's no secret?"

"Shit, no. He's asked everyone to go along with him. I don't think he's got many takers."

Anderson shook his head. "I thought he was really going to do it."

DeWeiss stopped before he left the building. "That's the strange thing. He might. I think he's just waiting for someone to say to him, 'Yeah, let's do it.' Why do you ask?"

"I guess because I'm his latest victim."

"Don't encourage him and he'll go off looking for someone else."

Anderson opened the door and stepped into the heat of the afternoon. "Shit," he said to himself.

EIGHT

ANDERSON handled all the details of flying back to Cu Chi from Saigon. He had to clear it with the tower at Tan Son Nhut, but now there was a Vietnamese controller on duty who kept telling Anderson to taxi but hold short of the runway. Anderson repeated that he was an Army Huey, six eight six, and that he wanted a departure from the Air America pad.

"You clear taxi to runway."

"Negative," said Anderson. "I'm a UH-1 helicopter and request departure from the Air American pad to the south."

"You taxi."

Anderson glanced at Brown, who was grinning broadly, enjoying the situation. Anderson reached down and turned the Fox Mike to Hotel Three.

"Hotel Three, this is Blackhawk six eight six, on the Air America pad with departure to the south. I cannot get the

117

Tan Son Nhut tower to understand that this is a helicopter and that I don't want to use the runway."

"Wait one."

Anderson leaned back in the seat and then pulled down the sun visor on his helmet. With the sun beating in through the windshield, it was suddenly hot in the helicopter. Sweat beaded and dripped and soaked Anderson's uniform. He pulled in a little pitch, trying to create a breeze with the rotor to cool them, but that didn't work.

"Six eight six, this is Hotel Three. You are cleared for takeoff. Climb out to the south. Call at five hundred feet."

"Roger." Anderson sucked in pitch, used the pedals, and pushed the cyclic forward, taking off. He paralleled the runway and then turned to the south. He keyed the mike. "Five hundred feet."

"Roger six eight six, say intentions."

"Depart traffic pattern to the south."

"Departure approved. Be advised of VFR traffic in your vicinity."

"Roger traffic. Thanks for the help."

They headed south to Highway One and then turned to the west following the road. Long before they could see the base at Cu Chi, they could see a column of smoke. Anderson wasn't sure what was happening on the northeastern side of the base, but there was always that column of smoke. If he'd been lost and within fifty miles of Cu Chi, he would have been able to find the camp because of the smoke. It was some kind of dump site where great quantities of waste were burned.

As they neared Cu Chi, Anderson called the tower and requested permission to land at POL. Permission was granted, and he set down at one of the refueling points. Brown leaped out to refuel the helicopter. That accomplished, they took off again and stayed in the traffic pattern, landing next to the runway and then hovering into the revetment area.

Anderson shut down and filled out the book while Brown

watched everything. When he had completed that, and the blade was tied down, Brown said, "Nice job."

"Thanks."

"That was good thinking when you called Hotel Three to get clearance. Showed that you had enough smarts to make the system work for you."

"I would like to say that I think it's marvelous that we give the Vietnamese an opportunity to work. Maybe next time they could hire someone who actually speaks English."

Brown opened his door and dropped his flight helmet to the ground. He donned his soft cap and said, "Treaty arrangements with the South Vietnamese require that we hire them to work."

"I understand that," said Anderson. "I was only suggesting that they hire someone who could speak our language."

Brown nodded and then went on. "Only thing I can fault you for was the landing at the Air America pad."

"Yeah," agreed Anderson. "That was sloppy, but as you said, switching seats can mess you up."

"Anyway, I think you'll be flying as a PPIC until we can get this AC problem solved."

"Okay," said Anderson. "I sure as hell hope you know what you're doing."

Now Brown laughed. "I don't know what I might have said to make you think I knew what I was doing. We're just all stumbling around trying not to get killed."

Anderson reached down and opened his door. He climbed out of the helicopter and then stopped. At the VIP pad he saw nearly a hundred men lined up facing a single man who stood in the center, his head bent and a book held in his hand.

"Looks like they've started the memorial service already."

"We'd better hurry," said Brown.

Leaving their equipment in the cargo compartment, they slipped into the rear of the formation. The men stood with their heads bowed as the chaplain read from the book he held. In front of him was a row of boots to signify the fallen men. Steel pots sat in front of the boots. A light breeze was blowing, so that the champlain had to hold the page flat with one hand while he read in a monotone.

Anderson, at the rear of the formation, could hear nothing from the chaplain. There was the sound of helicopters operating around them. The roar of the turbines, and the popping of the rotors that came and went, drowned out everything.

The chaplain turned, waving one hand, as if gesturing at the sky. He shouted then, his voice lost in the pounding of a rotor, and when the helicopter was gone, the chaplain was speaking quietly again.

Anderson stared at the men around him. None of them could hear the chaplain's words and none of them seemed to care. Maybe they resented this outsider coming in and telling them about life and death and fighting wars. Maybe they resented the formality of a service held while they stood in ranks and let someone else lecture them. Maybe they resented being in Vietnam when it seemed that no one wanted them there except the president and Congress.

The chaplain finished and Major Fox stepped to the front. He stood quietly, head bowed as if praying, and then raised his voice. "We all lost friends last night. Good friends—and there is a tendency to mourn that loss. But we shouldn't. They died in a good cause, helping others to remain free. They died doing something they believed in, and if there is a just God in the heavens above us, they are all with Him now."

That last was something that Anderson couldn't take. He wanted to shout at Fox, tell him that he was full of shit, but knew that this wasn't the place. Instead, he turned, walking back toward the aircraft.

Doing something they believed in. Christ, what a joke. Almost everyone Anderson knew was in Vietnam involuntarily. Oh, many like him had volunteered to join the Army, but it was a way to beat the draft. The draftees had almost no choice in what they did or when they did it. The volunteers got to hope for a school other than infantry AIT and a combat job on the ground. Anderson's plan had been to miss the Vietnam War by spending a year in training. As the training and the year wound down, he realized that he had miscalculated, and like everyone else in his flight-school class he had ended up with orders for Vietnam.

Looking back, he realized that his mistake was not applying for college, where he could hide from the Army like so many of his friends. He had volunteered for the Army but wasn't thrilled with the orders for the war.

Now he was being told that they were fighting for democracy in Southeast Asia and that his friends had died for a cause they believed in. What utter crap. They had died because they had the bad luck to step in front of, or fly in front of, a bullet. They didn't believe in the South Vietnamese. Most of them hated the South Vietnamese because they were thieves, cowards, and liars. They respected the enemy because he would fight, but not the South Vietnamese.

Anderson climbed into the cargo compartment of the helicopter. Through the windshield, he could see that Fox was still talking to the troops. That was another thing that Anderson had noticed. Fox loved to stand in front of the men and talk about anything. He stretched meetings to the breaking point and now was doing the same with the memorial service.

It all seemed unfair—kids in the World protesting the war but never understanding a thing about it; the press reporting on it, but never venturing out with the troops to see what it was like. Everyone seemed to have the answers to all the questions about the war, except the men who were fighting and dying in it.

Anderson felt the tears come then—a burning in his eyes that angered him. It wasn't that he wanted to hide his feelings. It just seemed wrong to be crying for the dead men, just as it had seemed wrong to be standing in the Gunfighter's Club watching the naked woman dance. Somewhere in the middle was where he should be, but the Saturday matinees and John Wayne hadn't taught him that.

War was glorified in those movies, but the death was overlooked. Somehow John Wayne dying at the end of *The Sands of Iwo Jima* had seemed right. A single, neat bullet hole and a tidy ending. In real life it wasn't that way and Hollywood and school and the Army all failed to teach him how to react or how to feel. No one ever got killed in war, except that they did, and the parody of a memorial service that he had just witnessed seemed to underscore the whole ludicrous system, in which men used the deaths of others for their own glory.

Anderson wiped his eyes with the sleeve of his jungle fatigues and took a deep breath. What he wanted to do was get drunk. Rip-roaring, falling-down, nasty drunk. So drunk that they had to carry him from the club. So drunk that he would have no idea about what he'd done. One night of total oblivion before he had to get back into the air and fly for the greater glory of LBJ and Nguyen Van Thieu.

"You ready to talk about that mission now?" asked a voice.

Anderson turned and saw that Sadler had slipped away from the memorial service. "I don't know."

"It's getting close to the time when we should do it. I DEROS in a few weeks, and if we don't get it lined up, we won't have the opportunity."

Anderson remembered what DeWeiss had told him about Sadler being slightly off center. It was strange that Sadler would approach him only a couple of hours after that discussion.

"Well?"

Anderson glanced out the window and saw that the memorial service was breaking up. Fox was standing in the center of the pad, shaking hands with the chaplain. That seemed strange—two men standing together, probably congratulating each other on a job well done, while others went home in metal boxes.

"I don't know," repeated Anderson.

"Look, we don't have much time. I thought you had a mind of your own and could see through the bullshit. See what had to be done."

"That doesn't mean that this is something that I should be doing."

Sadler climbed up into the cargo compartment and crouched. He looked like a Vietnamese peasant, squatting in a field. "We play all these games. We obey imaginary lines on the ground while the enemy ignores them. We watch friends die and then hold services so that others will feel better. We do nothing to end this nonsense because men in Washington don't want it to end yet. The time isn't right."

"Man," said Anderson, "I am not ready for this. I am just not ready."

Sadler nodded wisely and then stepped down to the dirt beside the helicopter. "I can understand that. I was just checking. When you're ready, you come and see me. Now that you're a PPIC, things will be easier."

As Sadler turned to leave, Anderson said, "Wait. How many others have said they'd go?"

"When you're ready, I'll let you know more. Right now is not the time." Sadler left then.

Anderson sat there for a long time. The sky slowly darkened and the airfield, except for the tiny, dim lines along the runway, turned black. The sounds of aircraft operating, the stench of the JP-4 burning, began to fade as it got later. Anderson lost track of the time. Lost track of everything.

Finally he realized that he was thirsty. He picked up his gear and headed back toward the company area.

The officers' club was filled with people, but there wasn't the corresponding noise level. It was subdued in the club, the men talking in muted tones. There were a few women scattered around—nurses from the Twelfth Evac Hospital down the road. Two of them wore jungle fatigues, but the rest had changed into civilian clothes. Strangely, the men were not clustered around them as would have been usual.

Anderson entered and stepped to the bar. "Give me a bourbon and Coke."

The bartender nodded and disappeared for a moment. He came back and set the drink in front of Anderson, waving off the money. "Harned was afraid of something happening and left two hundred dollars to buy the bar in case he didn't return."

"Well that's just fucking wonderful," said Anderson. He couldn't understand where his anger was coming from. If Harned wanted to buy the bar, it was his privilege, even if he was dead.

Anderson took the drink and drifted into the crowd. He stood on the outside of a circle of men and listened while they discussed the end of the baseball season. That was something that no one had ever taken an interest in. Who had cared what the baseball teams were doing twelve thousand miles away? Somehow it was hard to generate any enthusiasm for a kid's game played by men when it was impossible to get the scores for days. Now everyone was interested in the pennant races. The man from Chicago was claiming that the Cubs would not take their annual nose-dive in August.

Anderson drained his drink and headed back to the bar for another. This time he ordered two and then walked around the exterior wall of the building until he found a vacant table. He dropped into the chair, gulped one of the drinks, and set the empty glass on the table.

Baseball, for Christ's sake. Next they would be discussing politics and the home front, where the civilian population did everything they could to prolong the war and give aid and comfort to the enemy. Didn't the assholes realize that the communists read newspapers and watched television? Student riots in the World weren't helping end the war. There was no reason for the North Vietnamese to negotiate if the American people were going to give everything away anyway.

Maybe that was where the anger was coming from. Not from Harned buying the bar because he thought he was going to die, but from realizing that the people at home didn't care that Harned had died. His family would suffer, and they would receive the hate mail telling his mother that it was good that he had died. One less capitalist pig trying to subjugate the Oriental and free people of Southeast Asia.

This was doing him no good, he suddenly realized. He had to do something more than sit on his butt worrying about people in the World who had no idea what was happening in Vietnam. All they ever saw was the bullshit put out by the networks, by biased reporters who worked to get the story they wanted, which was not necessarily the truth, yet not necessarily lies either. It was a slanted, tainted view that too many people accepted without asking a few simple questions.

Anderson had seen the now world-famous photograph of the chief of the Saigon police gunning down the VC in the city's streets. He had watched the whole horrible show as it was played over and over on the news, but not one reporter told the complete story. Not one explained that the man shot had just killed the family of a Saigon policeman. No one was interested in the fact the man had murdered a woman and her kids. They only saw the shooting in the streets of Saigon and refused to understand it.

Anderson felt his blood boil. Good men were dying all over South Vietnam so that people at home could collect supplies for the enemy. Noncombat aid. Medicine and food and clothes, shipped to North Vietnam in the name of peace. Except those medicines and food and clothes were used by the North Vietnamese Army to help them fight the war. Maybe that kind of help was not as lethal as bullets and rifles, but it helped the enemy keep the war going nonetheless.

He picked up his second drink and gulped it down too, but

he didn't feel the warming buzz that too much alcohol too fast usually gave him. There was no pleasant sensation of floating and no tingling of the skin on his face. Just a white-hot anger building in his gut as he thought of all the stupidity that had led to the night before. Too many people making too many decisions without thinking about all the consequences.

The chair across from his scraped on the plywood floor and one of the nurses sat down. She stared at him and said, "You seem awfully quiet."

Anderson tried to smile, but it felt wrong, as if he were sneering at her. He didn't feel like talking to anyone, but realized that if he sat there, drinking and letting his mind wander, he was going to get into a homicidal mood.

The nurse looked to be nearly as young as he was. She had long blond hair that hung down her back and was cut in bangs. It had to be murder trying to keep it clean and to meet Army regulations which would force her to pile it up while in uniform. She had a long face and big dark eyes. She smiled and said, "Hey. Hello."

"Hello," said Anderson. "Sorry." He waved a hand around and added, "It's been a bad day."

"For us too," said the woman.

Anderson was about to ask how it could be bad for those who stayed behind at the base camp all the time, but then knew how it could be bad. They would get the unpleasant task of cleaning up the mess, trying to fix the broken and shot-up bodies brought to them. Maybe if she had been a clerk who sat in a bunker all day, it would have been good duty, but he knew that working in the hospital could be as bad as flying in the war.

"Then maybe I should buy you a drink," said Anderson.

"No," she said. "I think that I should buy you one. You look like you could use it more than I could."

"In flight school we were taught to never turn down free drinks. Bourbon and Coke."

She got up and moved into the crowd, heading toward the

bar. As she did, Anderson's mind seemed to go blank. The anger that he had been feeling evaporated in an instant. He smiled to himself and knew that it was the woman. Just the fact that she had noticed him and felt enough compassion to speak to him seemed to take the edge off his anger.

She returned and set the drink in front of him. Then she held out a hand and said, "I'm Sandy."

"David Anderson, though they call me Andy here."

"You say that like this is the only place they call you that."

"Exactly. At home I was always Alex, which is my middle name."

"Must get confusing." She sat down again.

"Not really, and besides, here they also give you a call sign."

"So, David, Andy, or whoever, what would you like to talk about?"

"Anything but the war."

"No problem there. What'd you do before you ended up here?"

"I was a high-school student."

She looked at him through hooded eyes and asked, "Just how old are you anyway?"

"Nineteen."

"Christ, they're robbing the cradles for their cannon fodder."

"You don't look to be that much older," said Anderson.

"I'm twenty-three, and let me tell you, it's a world of difference between nineteen and twenty-three."

Anderson picked up his glass and sipped his drink. It was now no longer important for him to get drunk. The need for oblivion had passed.

"Thanks," he said.

"For what?"

"The drink. Sitting down. Just being here at the right moment to say the right thing, though I suspect the right thing would have been anything."

"You sure you're only nineteen?"

"I could show you my ID card with my date of birth on it."

"You know, I thought you had to have some college just to get in the military flight programs."

"That's if you want to be a real pilot and fly with the Air Force or the Navy. In the Army we have aviators, and they'll take anyone with a little intelligence and a warm body. As you said, they need cannon fodder."

"I didn't mean it quite like that."

Anderson laughed. It was a single bark. "But I did because it fits so perfectly. It's exactly what we are. Too unimportant to worry about, but someone to do the job until the politicians decide that it's time to end the war. Then we all go home."

"I really didn't mean anything by it."

Anderson leaned forward and touched her arm. "I know, and that might be the saddest thing of all."

NINE

ANDERSON was sure that he had overslept when the wake officer passed through his hootch, getting the pilots out of bed. It was a good thirty minutes later than it should have been, and although his head ached and his mouth tasted as if it were full of bird droppings, he leaped up. He grabbed his bottle of mouthwash and took a healthy slug of it, sloshing it around and then swallowing it.

He threw on his uniform and grabbed his helmet and weapon and then his chicken plate. Without eating, he rushed to operations to check the aircraft assignments, and as he looked up at the board, realized that he was in command of the aircraft—not as an AC, but still in command, which meant that his copilot was out on the line doing the preflight.

He relaxed then, signing out the SOI and walking slowly up the stairs. It wasn't that he was late—actually he was early. He could go to the mess hall for a glass of juice or some breakfast, or he could head on out to the flight line. Breakfast was the last thing he wanted, so he walked to the flight line. He knew that if he waited, there would be a jeep or a truck along to drive him. It was one of the benefits of leaving the ranks of the Peter Pilot.

He found his aircraft and saw Jones, his scheduled copilot, crawling over the head, checking it closely. Anderson didn't know that much about Jones. He'd been in-country for about ten weeks, but had been assigned to the First Platoon, which meant that Anderson saw him but rarely talked to him. Now it seemed that he was going to be flying in the Second Platoon.

Jones was so recently in-country that he was still impressed with the fact that they let him wear a pistol all the time, and he couldn't help playing with it. He was a short man with dark hair and a bad sunburn. He was nervous, shifting his weight from one foot to the other.

Anderson tossed his gear into the cargo compartment and then said to Jones. "You check the book?"

"Of course. Windshield is scratched, which means we're not supposed to fly at night, but other than that, everything is fine."

"How'd the preflight go?"

"Everything looks good," said Jones. He crouched down, an arm across a knee. "I've finished up here unless you want to take a look."

"No," said Anderson. "I'm sure it's fine. Hell, you're flying in this too."

And even though Anderson said that, he remembered that most of the ACs had checked the head anyway. Anderson hadn't liked it when they did, because it meant they didn't trust him to do it right, but they never found anything that he'd missed. He decided that Jones, trained in the same school that he'd gone to, would know enough to find anything that was wrong.

Jones climbed down the opposite side of the helicopter

and then came around to talk. "What's laid on for this morning?"

Anderson had to shrug. If there had been an ACs meeting the night before, he hadn't been asked to attend. They usually met for twenty minutes and were given the preliminaries for the next day's missions, which didn't necessarily mean that the information would be right or current by the time they took off the next morning. Often, night activities changed the schedule.

"I think," said Anderson, "that we had nothing scheduled for today until Major Fox could assure the battalion CO that we could put up a flight."

"Volunteering us for more important missions?"

Anderson wasn't sure that he liked the tone of Jones's voice, but then, he wasn't sure that he liked Fox volunteering them for missions either. Especially while he orbited at three thousand feet watching the war being fought.

"Why don't you get commo check made?"

"Sure," said Jones. He climbed into his side of the aircraft, flipped on the battery switch, and then the radios. He put on his helmet and reached up to squeeze the mike button on the cyclic.

Anderson got into the back and sat down on the troopseat. He hung his head and stared at the gray metal floor of the cargo compartment. He wasn't concerned about the upcoming missions, because he knew that he would be in the center of the flight, protected by everyone else. The others would be watching out for him. All he had to do was the job he'd been trained to do, over five hundred hours of flight time.

He looked up and saw that Jones had shut down the radios and was sitting there, watching the sun rise as the rest of the pilots, the crew chiefs, and the gunners filtered into the revetment area.

Then, before he had a chance to worry about much of anything, the rotating beacon of the lead aircraft came on as the signal for the others to crank. Anderson slipped into his chicken plate, plugged his helmet into the radio-intercom system, and climbed into his seat.

He touched the floor button and said, "Go ahead and wind it up."

Jones used the laminated card to run through the checklist, and then turned on the battery, the start fuel, and the start generator. Anderson watched it all but didn't comment. He didn't have anything to say.

When the aircraft was running Anderson said, "Okay, I've got it."

"You've got it."

Anderson keyed the mike and told lead that they were up. The call was rogered and, a few moments later, lead announced that he was taking off.

The morning mission was easy. They lifted grunts from a PZ near a fire-support base to an LZ that was a wide-open field with the closest trees over a hundred yards away. The second lift was as easy as the first, and Anderson let Jones fly it. They returned to Cu Chi, refueled, and then took another company out into the war. When that was done, they returned and shut down, standing by on the aircraft for thirty minutes. Finally the operations clerk came out and told them that they could wait in the company area.

They had a hot lunch in the mess hall and then returned to their hootches. Jones had stayed close to Anderson until then, but returned to his own hootch. Anderson turned on the TV to watch the reruns of the programs shown the night before. AFVN came on the air about thirteen hundred.

They had watched half an episode of *Combat!* when the PA announced, "All flight crews report to their aircraft. Pilots report to operations."

"Shit," said Anderson. "Now I won't find out if Sarge will survive until next week."

"Don't worry," said Timberlake. "I'll watch closely and let you know."

Anderson grabbed his cap and pistol and headed for operations to learn what new mission Fox had volunteered them for.

Coming out of operations, later in the afternoon, Anderson stopped and stared at the road. A black, foul-smelling, semiliquid mess had been poured all over it to hold down the dust.

Timberlake came up the steps and stopped next to Anderson. "Well, shit. Peta-prime."

"Just what in the hell is peta-prime?"

"I'm not sure," said Timberlake, "but I think it has something to do with the communist attempt to win the war. They sneak in during the night and spread it all over the countryside. The sages in intel claim that peta-prime is an oil-based tar that holds the dust down, but I know better. The communists do it to fuck with us."

"So what's the problem?" asked Jones.

"Problem?" asked Timberlake. "Problem? Just try to walk across that shit. It never dries. It stays in its semifluid state, sticking to everything. Boots. Clothes. Paper. The aircraft. You walk on it, and your boots collect a layer of it. Then you walk on the dirt and collect a layer of that. Back and forth until you're twelve feet tall. It sticks to the pedals in the aircraft and your feet stick to the pedals. It's all a communist plot. Trust me."

They moved down to the road. Timberlake pushed a toe into the black mass, as if he were testing the temperature of water before he jumped in. "Yup. Just as disgusting as ever."

Across the road the flight leader sat in the cargo compartment of his chopper, scraping at his jungle boots, trying to get the peta-prime off them. He glanced up and saw them standing there. He shouted at them, "You people want to get started, or you want to just stand there."

Timberlake was not intimidated. "I'll just stand here if that's really a choice."

Anderson slapped Jones on the shoulder. "Let's get going."

At the aircraft, the crew chief was trying to get the peta-prime off his boots. Anderson pointed to him and said to Jones, "That's Bauman. The door gunner, Trice, should be around some place."

Bauman hopped up and said, "They still haven't checked on that high-frequency vibration. I complained to maintenance, but they said we'd have to wait. They had too much other work to worry about a little vibration. If an aircraft is flyable, they're not going to fuck with it."

Anderson jumped into the cargo compartment so that he could get the book, leaving black footprints behind him. He flipped it open and saw that maintenance had signed off the write-up without fixing the problem. He crammed the book back into the map case and said, "If that's the way they want to handle it, then we're in the clear."

"Unless we crash and burn," said Bauman.

"They still won't come to us," said Anderson. He got out of the Huey and said to Jones, "Make a quick check of the bottom and I'll check the head."

"Yes, sir." Then Jones remembered that he was no longer in flight school and didn't have to call Anderson *sir*. He wished he could bite his tongue.

Anderson just ignored that. He knew that Jones would quickly get over it. Forgetting that he had told Jones that he trusted him, Anderson climbed to the top of the helicopter and began a systematic check. He worked his way through it, finishing by trying to twist off the Jesus nut, but it wouldn't turn. That was the huge nut that held the rotor system in place and was supposed to be torqued down so that there would be no way that it could be twisted, but Anderson habitually tried.

Finished, he sat down by the turbine and slid to the ground. He opened the door on his side of the aircraft and flipped on the battery switch. He checked the fuel level and a couple of the gauges.

Jones climbed into the other side and strapped in, glancing at Anderson out of the corner of his eyes because he'd checked the head, and began to run through the start procedure carefully. When he got to the point of having to start the engine, he looked at Anderson, who nodded. Jones turned to his right and yelled, "Clear!" He then squeezed the trigger under the throttle, starting the engine.

"Make the commo check," said Anderson.

That accomplished, they hovered out of the revetment and joined the flight as it lined up near the runway. Lead advised them that he was on the go, and the flight lifted off in sequence. They flew to the PZ, where they landed and shut down, told that they would extract a company of Vietnamese rangers in about an hour.

They took off, climbing into the hills. They came over them, descending to the tops of the scrub brush and dwarf trees. In the clearing in front of them, a cloud of red smoke erupted from the north side of the LZ.

Below them, Anderson could see the Vietnamese standing there, waiting for the flight. But there was no place to touch down—the clearing was littered with broken trees and tall thorn bushes.

There was an abrupt rattling from a single weapon. "Chock two is taking fire on the right." One of the gunships dived from the rear of the flight, its miniguns firing with the sound of a loud buzz saw.

"Shit," said Jones, ducking down.

"That's our guy," said Anderson calmly. He wasn't worried about a single weapon. Not after the night mission, where two hundred VC hadn't been able to kill him.

He shot to a hover, keeping the skids just out of the brush. Unfortunately, he was too high, and he tried to settle lower so that the Vietnamese could climb on. Off to the left there was a bright flash and the crump of an explosion.

"Flight's taking mortars," said one of the pilots. As always the voice was calm.

"Shit," said Jones.

Then, almost as if someone had shouted a command, the Vietnamese began scrambling over each other, trying to get into the helicopters. There were too many for a single load, meaning some would have to stay until there was a second lift. But their discipline disintegrated as the mortar shells continued to fall and small arms began to rattle.

"Flight's taking fire on the left."

There was shouting and screaming. One man punched another in the face. That man tumbled from the rear of a Huey. Another Vietnamese was swinging his rifle like a club.

Over the intercom, Anderson shouted, "Bauman, we're only taking nine. You keep the others off."

Bauman didn't answer. There was a commotion in the cargo compartment, and the aircraft rocked. There was a jerking at the skids, as five Vietnamese fought each other trying to get on. Two Vietnamese fell out of the helicopter. One landed flat on his back and didn't get up.

More shells were falling, but they were landing at the edge of the LZ, away from the flight. Firing broke out. AKs in the trees and M-16s in the LZ. The gunships rolled in, rockets or miniguns firing.

"We've got twelve," said Bauman. "They keep grabbing the skids. Can you pick up a little?"

Anderson began to suck in pitch, watching the torque meter climb toward the top, and ignoring the noise around him. More weapons began to fire. Shells continued to fall.

"Flight's taking fire on the left."

"Lead, you're down and loaded. Fire reported left and right. Mortars on the left."

"Lead's on the go."

"Lead, this is three six. We have movement in the trees in front of you."

"Roger."

One at a time the aircraft began picking up, and dumping their noses to make a run at the tree line at the far end of the LZ. As each one reached the trees, its AC would pop the collective, gaining enough altitude to clear the trees, but then using them for cover. The terrain and the density altitude demanded that the choppers fly out that way.

Lead made it easily, clearing the trees and climbing out to the left. Chock two had no problem. Chock three started to climb out, then broke to the right, down the mountainside, as if he had suddenly lost power and was trying to gain it back. Chock four followed lead's path, and Anderson followed him.

Charlie had been waiting while he tracked the first couple of Hueys. He waited for Anderson to clear the trees and opened fire again. Anderson felt the bullets rip into the bottom of the helicopter. He keyed the mike and said, "Chock five is taking fire from the left."

Through the earphones he heard a squeal as the Fox Mike began to disintegrate and cycle itself, looking for a frequency that it couldn't find. When the tuning squeal didn't stop, Anderson reached over and turned it off. He shot a glance at Jones, who was sitting bolt upright, almost as if he had been chiseled out of stone. He didn't move as Anderson dived for the ground, trying to avoid the enemy fire.

Over the radio he heard someone saying, "The AC's dead. The AC's dead." He wondered who had been killed now, and didn't know that it was Jones talking about him.

He had no time to worry about it, because the throttle linkage fell apart and the governor failed. The engine began to overspeed. Anderson fought for control, but there were too many other things wrong.

Out of the corner of his eye, he saw the flight begin to break up, as the others tried to get away from the sheet of lead that the VC were throwing into the sky. Anderson felt the rounds striking, tearing into the thin metal and destroying the Plexiglas.

For a moment it looked good. He had gotten things stabilized and thought that he could make it to the staging area. He was manually operating the throttle, and the engine instruments were in the green. There were no warning lights.

He started a gentle turn to the right, toward the rest of the flight. He relaxed slightly, letting the tension drain from his muscles. Just a few minutes and he would be in the clear. A few minutes more.

The burst from the concealed .50-caliber caught him by surprise. The first rounds smashed through the cargo compartment, killing five of the rangers. The bullets walked their way back, slamming through the transmission and the engine, destroying them. With a scream that sounded as if it had come from a mortally wounded rabbit, the engine died.

"Shit," said Anderson. He slammed down the collective and kicked at the pedals. "Chock five is going down, north-northwest of the Lima Zulu."

He tried to lengthen the glide, adding a little pitch so that he could clear a final row of trees. In the fading sunlight, he could see a series of rice paddies and aimed for them. He needed a little more pitch and, as he pulled it in, he knew that he had used too much when he had tried to extend the glide too far. He felt the sweat on his body and his heart in his chest. He knew that they were going to crash and that there was nothing he could do about it.

The right skid hit the top of a tree, and Anderson couldn't recover. The chopper began to spin, and he crammed in the right pedal, but it wasn't enough. The Huey hit low on its right side, bounced into the air, spilling out one body and two of the living Vietnamese, and smashed back to the ground, landing on its right side. Water splashed high into the air. There was a hissing as water hit the turbine. A cloud of steam and smoke rolled upward. Then there was no sound except for the bubbling of water as it tried to reclaim its lost territory. A second later someone screamed, "I'm shot."

Something changed then. There was shouting and screaming. Anderson tried to key the mike, but the radios were all dead. He released the cyclic and discovered that he had broken the plastic grip.

There was the sound of scrambling as the last living Vietnamese ranger tried to get out. He jumped into the rice paddy and ran for the trees, leaving everything—his rifle, helmet, equipment—behind him. He didn't care.

Again the voice from the rear came. "Please. Help me. I'm shot."

Anderson, wedged into his seat, put one hand on the console to support himself. He unbuckled his seat belt and fell slightly. As he put out one knee, he levered himself backward and cleared the seat. He fell through empty air, dropping to the ground and landing in rice paddy's water. For a moment he struggled like a turtle on its back, finally clawing his way to a sitting position. He turned and stared into the half-submerged face of the door gunner.

The man was dead. There was no life in the one staring eye that Anderson could see. The transmission had ripped itself out of the aircraft on impact and crushed him.

Now Anderson stood up, knee-deep in the water. He was still inside the aircraft, which lay on its side. In the other well, Bauman was lying on his back, his legs in the air. He had both hands pressed against his chest holding tightly to the chicken plate.

Anderson moved to him. "It's okay. We'll get you out of here."

He looked over his shoulder and saw Jones struggling to get out. He had managed to stand, and was trying to open the door on what was now the top of the aircraft. Anderson said, "You all right?"

"Yeah. Fine."

Reaching for the crew chief's seat belt, Anderson said, "Crawl over here and we'll try to lift him out. We'll have to be careful. I don't know how badly hurt he is."

"What about the door gunner?"

"He's dead. So are the Vietnamese."

Together, with Anderson on the inside and Jones on the outside, they lifted the crew chief up and over, laying him on the cargo door. Then Jones helped Anderson out and, after he had dropped to the ground, Jones handed the wounded man down to him. They leaned Bauman against the top of the aircraft. Anderson pulled the Velcro strips that unfastened the chicken plate, so that he could remove it.

When it was free, Anderson took one look and turned his head, clamping his teeth so that he wouldn't throw up. He took a deep breath and then a second. When he was in control again, he said, "Get the first-aid kit."

By now it was practically dark. Overhead, to the northwest, he could see helicopters working over the enemy positions, while others looked for the downed aircraft. There was the distant sound of firing, and tracers flashed in the late-evening sky like fireworks gone berserk.

Before the light was completely gone, he ripped open Bauman's fatigue shirt and pulled it away from the wound. The bullet had apparently entered from the side, where there was no protection, and burst out the front of the chest on the opposite side. Anderson was no medic, but he had been taught enough to recognize a sucking chest wound when he saw it. There was so much blood that he couldn't believe that Bauman was still alive.

"We've got to get out of here, " said Jones. His voice was raw, as if he had been shouting.

Anderson ignored that as Bauman became delirious. He was talking in a ragged voice about being cold, terribly cold. There were bright lights from the New Year's Eve parties. Bauman laughed then, saying that he had drunk too much. The laugh turned into a gurgling cough as blood dribbled down his chin. With a shaky hand he rubbed it away.

Anderson sat down in the water and pulled Bauman toward him, propping him up so that his head and chest were out of the dirty water. Not that it would matter much longer.

Jones crouched near him and handed him the first-aid kit. "We've got to get out of here."

"Later," said Anderson. He shook the large bandage out and tried to apply it to the wound. He pressed it tight so that Bauman could breathe more easily.

Bauman was whimpering. Once he shouted but there were no words. Only unintelligible sounds. Anderson leaned down and whispered in his ear. "Quiet. We have to be quiet."

"How is he?" asked Jones.

Anderson looked into Jones's eyes and shook his head. Out loud he said, "He'll be fine just as soon as we can get him to a doctor."

In the distance rattled the sounds of automatic weapons, artillery, and rockets. Tracers, both red and green, were bouncing all over. Anderson knew that people were looking for them. People on both sides. To be safe, they had to get away from the Huey, but they couldn't move because Bauman would die if they tried to move him. He was going to die anyway, Anderson knew, but he couldn't leave the man. And he couldn't do anything to kill him.

"Where's the survival radio?" Anderson asked, trying to think his way through the problem.

Jones shook his head. "Lost it in the water. I don't know where it is."

"Check the perimeter," said Anderson. They didn't have a perimeter, but Jones could look around. It would keep him busy for a moment.

Bauman began to moan, quietly at first and then louder. Anderson wanted to clamp a hand over his mouth, but couldn't. One was holding the bandage in place, and the other was supporting Bauman so that he wouldn't slip into the water.

"I'm cold," he said. "Oh, my God! I'm paralyzed."

"No," whispered Anderson. "We're in the water. It's the water that's cold. You're going to be all right. You're going to be fine."

"It hurts, sir. Hurts bad."

"I know. Hold on, we're doing everything we can." Anderson kept talking, saying whatever came into his mind, because he didn't know what to tell Bauman. He kept his voice low, aware that the enemy was out there somewhere looking for them, but the sound of his voice seemed to soothe Bauman. The man relaxed when he heard it. He had accepted everything and was now waiting for Anderson to do something to get them out.

But all Anderson could do was pray that Bauman would hurry up and die so that he could get out of there. Every second that he stayed meant it was more likely that the VC would come, and the VC didn't take helicopter pilots as prisoners. They killed them. As horribly as they could. So Anderson wanted the crew chief to die, the ordeal to end. He was powerless to do anything to end it. He could only sit in the cold, dirty water of the rice paddy and stare into the inky blackness of the night, wishing that Bauman would die.

Bauman was holding his own. He was complaining about the cold. Then he slipped into dreams that clouded his thinking. He screamed something that sounded like, "Drinks on the house." Then he struggled to sit up, turned his head, and said, quite clearly, "Jeez, it's cold."

"I know it," said Anderson. "I think it might snow." To himself, he kept saying, "Hurry up and die."

At that moment, Anderson wasn't aware of what he was saying. He felt slightly sick from having a hand pressed into the gore that had been his friend's chest. His legs were going to sleep from having Bauman lying on them. And he was scared now, as scared as he had ever been in Vietnam, because he knew that Charlie was out there somewhere, trying to find him. He didn't want to be captured and had often claimed that he wouldn't be, if he was conscious. But now that seemed like bravado, because he was no longer sure that he could shoot himself as he had said that he would. He would shoot at the VC, but if they wanted to take him alive, he was fairly sure that they could do it. Besides, after having sat in the water, he was no longer sure that his pistol would fire.

He didn't care about that. All he wanted was for Bauman to die so he could get out of there. He wanted him to do it quickly, and wondered how he could help him die without seeming to help.

Jones came back, keeping low. He crouched close to Anderson and said, "I think there are some people moving around out there. I don't know who they are."

"Well, shit," said Anderson. "We've got to get out of here." He tried to ease Bauman off him.

Bauman reached out and grabbed Anderson's collar. In a clear voice, only slightly furred by pain, he said, "You cannot leave me, Andy. It would not be right."

"I'm not going to leave you," said Anderson. "I'm trying to make you more comfortable."

Bauman began to let go of the cloth, but then jerked once, dragging Anderson's face toward him as he spasmed and died. The death rattle, a noise deep in his throat as the last of the air escaped his lungs, burst into Anderson's face. He could smell the blood and death and wanted again to throw up, but forced himself not to. Angrily, he pushed Bauman away from him. He wiped his hands on his own fatigues.

Jones reached out to help him stand up, but Anderson slapped the hand away. "Don't touch me."

Before they could move, a helicopter flew over them and flashed its landing light. There was no fire from the VC or the trees nearby. The pilot, believing that it was safe, returned and hovered only fifteen feet away.

Anderson bent his head forward into the wind from the rotorblades. The wind pulled water from the paddy, soaking him further, like spray from the ocean on a windy day.

As the Huey touched down, Anderson and Jones sprinted through the knee-deep water toward the waiting aircraft. They had not thought about removing the machine guns, zeroing the radios, taking the battery, or destroying the commo gear. Jones thought that it was Anderson's job, and Anderson was now too frightened to worry about it. All he could think of was getting out, away from the dead man and the Vietcong.

As they climbed into the waiting aircraft, the crew chief asked, "Where are the others?"

"Dead."

"Your equipment?" When he saw the look on Anderson's

face, he wished that he hadn't asked. He pushed the button on the intercom so that he could talk to the pilots. "That's it, sir. We can go."

Without a question, the AC pulled the pitch, did a pedal turn, and climbed out. Over the radio he said, "I've picked up the survivors. The aircraft is down, on its side in a rice paddy about three klicks north of the LZ. Suggest that the gun team blow it up."

"Roger one two."

On the way back to the base camp, Anderson didn't think about what had just happened. His mind was numb, floating from one thing to the next without logical progression. He was away from Vietnam. The crew chief noticed that Anderson kept rubbing his hands on the front of his fatigues, as if he was trying to get dirt off them.

At operations, he was told to fill out the hit report, in detail because people had been killed. Then he was told that someone from Battalion would want to talk to him in the morning, for some kind of survey they were running, but that it would wait until he had a chance to unwind and get cleaned up.

Outside, under the black Vietnamese sky, Anderson felt that something was wrong. At the moment, he didn't know what it was, but felt, somehow, that there should have been more to the questioning in operations. All they had asked was that he fill out the normal paperwork. They had, in essence, patted him on the head and told him to go relax. Two of his crew were dead. Not by his hand, but that didn't matter. They were dead and it seemed that something more should be done, if only to mark their passing. The whole thing seemed too routine now. Too remote. When a man died, someone should notice. Someone should try to determine why, so that it could be kept from happening again. He shouldn't be told to fill out papers and relax. They shouldn't hold memorial services on the flight line. Something more should be done.

He realized that this was at odds with what he had felt when he shot the VC. But that was different. Bauman and Trice were men that he knew. Men he had shared drinks with, joked with, and flown with. Anderson didn't care about the Vietnamese. He cared about Bauman and Trice.

Slowly he walked back toward the officer's area. From the club he could hear the sounds of laughter and the singing of a musical group started by a bunch of clerks at Battalion. They played each night in one of the many clubs that belonged to the units in the battalion. From somewhere else he could hear a TV. Ironically, Captain Kirk was lamenting the death of one of his security people. Play deaths had more emotion, more pain attached to them. The real deaths passed unnoticed.

But now, in Vietnam, Anderson didn't react, didn't cry. He didn't feel guilt. He didn't feel anything. And that bothered him. He new that he should feel something more than anger because operations hadn't wanted anything other than a hit report. But the war had been going on for so long, and so many people had died, that he could feel nothing, even if the most recent victim had died in his arms asking not to be left alone.

Maybe that was part of it. Anderson had left him—left him face down in the cold, dark water, the first chance he got. They could have recovered the body, but it had seemed ridiculous to waste the living on the dead. Both he and Jones had run, as soon as they had the chance.

The song ended, and several men left the hootch on their way to the club. When they saw Anderson, one of them said, "Hey, Andy, that was a rough one."

Anderson nodded. "Yeah. It sure was." He was surprised by his own voice. It sounded as if he had just left the dorm and was on his way to the movies or to visit a girl.

* * *

The next day, the horror of the night before was nearly buried in the routine. Since he had been involved in a crash, he couldn't fly until the flight surgeon had cleared him, and there was the survey that needed completing at Battalion. Anderson got the day down. A kind of reward for losing his aircraft.

TEN

ANDERSON spent the morning at Battalion running from one office to the next. He had to describe to the operations officer how he had gotten shot down, and then had to fill out another hit report detailing the damage to the aircraft. He met with the battalion commander, an older man with thinning hair, starched fatigues, and a perfect tan, who asked a dozen questions, half of which actually pertained to the incident. He visited another office, was given another form, and told to fill it out. When that was done, he was taken to see the chaplain, who talked about God and His mysterious ways, and how we aren't always privileged to know His greater plan.

Anderson stared at the man as if he were speaking a foreign language. He didn't want to hear about it, not after sitting in the rice paddy and feeling the life drain out of another man. The chaplain had nothing to say that Anderson wanted to hear, and although the man was a captain, Anderson walked out of the office without saying a word.

Finally, he was scheduled to see the flight surgeon at Battalion, who looked at him, shined a light in his eyes, and said, "No reason you can't fly. No reason for you to stay down."

"Thanks," said Anderson as he left. Naturally, there was no one around to give him a ride, so he had to walk back to the company area. Not a long walk, just a hot one with the mid-morning sun pounding down on him. Sweat blossomed and dripped, and he was thirsty, but it was better to walk down the roads at Cu Chi than to try forcing his way through the jungle outside the wire.

At the company area, he went immediately to the officers' club and ordered a beer. He drank it in three quick gulps and then ordered a second.

Brown came by, saw him, and stopped to ask, "How you doing today?"

"Just fine, Captain. Completed the paperwork and interviews at Battalion, and their flight surgeon has cleared me to fly."

"Good. Why don't you swing by to see our doc when you get a chance? He'll need to certify that the crash didn't harm you."

"Oh, it's a crash now, is it?"

"You have to admit that the aircraft crashed," said Brown.

"That means there's going to be a survey to determine whether I was at fault for the crash. Pilot flew into hostile fire and crashed. Obviously pilot error."

Brown climbed onto the stool next to Anderson and pointed at the bartender. When he had a beer, he said, "You know that it's not going to be like that."

"After everything that has happened in the last week, I wouldn't be surprised at anything they throw at us."

"Maybe you should put in for your R and R now. Take a week of rest."

"Right," said Anderson. "We're short of pilots but the solution is to send me on R and R."

Brown took a deep drink of his beer and said, "I thought that for your mental health, it might be the thing to do."

"If you're worried about my mental health, three days in Saigon would work just fine."

"I'll check with Major Fox and get back to you on that."

"You do that," said Anderson. He watched as Brown retreated then, leaving his beer on the bar. "Christ, how in the hell can we win a war with fucking managers? We need leaders, not corporate types who think managing is leading."

"You say something?" asked the bartender.

"No, not a thing. " Anderson got off his stool and left the club, heading toward his hootch. Before he got there, he changed direction, heading toward operations. He entered, walked down the stairs, and then around to the back where Sadler spent most of the day.

Sadler was sitting there, reading a report. He looked up when Anderson approached but didn't speak.

"It's time," said Anderson.

"All right," said Sadler. "I'll be by your hootch tonight about nineteen hundred. We'll get the ball rolling then."

Anderson hesitated, staring at the other man, but could think of nothing more to say. He turned and retreated, in much the same manner that Brown had, a couple of minutes earlier.

Anderson was sitting on his bunk when Sadler appeared in the doorway. Sadler nodded and said, "Are you ready?"

"We going so soon?"

"There are some preliminaries that we have to take care of first. We're not even leaving the base camp tonight."

Anderson remembered how mad Brown had gotten the time that he had flown out with the maintenance officer. He knew that he really couldn't tell Brown where he would be, because it would lead to a dozen questions that he couldn't answer.

"What do I tell Brown?"

"You leave that to me. I'll handle him. Let's go."

Anderson grabbed his cap and followed Sadler out of the hootch. They walked down to the open area where the company vehicles were parked. Sadler got behind the wheel of the one that said OPERATIONS on the white strip painted under the windshield.

As he started the jeep, Sadler said, "Tonight is the preliminaries. We get everything arranged for tomorrow night."

"Then you have enough pilots," said Anderson.

"With you, yes. I also have crew chiefs and gunners. All we have to do is file the serial numbers off the rockets."

They pulled out onto the dirt road and then turned toward the perimeter.

"I've been going to ask you about that," said Anderson. "Why bother filing the numbers off the rockets?"

"So they can't be traced to us."

"Hell, everyone and his brother is going to know that it was the Americans who did it."

Sadler slowed and flipped on the blackout lights of the jeep. He turned onto the road that was inside the bunker line and headed in the direction of the rearm point, which was close to the refueling point.

"Sure they'll know that it was the Americans, but without the serial numbers, they won't have proof. They'll have some shrapnel that won't prove a thing. If there were serial numbers that somehow survived, then some smart-ass reporter might be able to trace them to our rearm point. Without the numbers, they won't have a starting point."

Anderson shrugged, not sure that it made any difference at all, but if Sadler wanted to take the precaution of filing the numbers off the rockets, then he'd help.

"I've spent two months reading the various intelligence reports coming from all over." Sadler shot him a glance and grinned. "We're talking CIA and DIA and the Special Forces and even the Navy's SEALs."

"What are the SEALs?" asked Anderson.

"They're a classified unit in the Navy that goes out and does secret shit all over the place. Navy won't even admit they exist. But I've gotten a couple of their reports too."

"And these reports?" prompted Anderson.

"These reports pinpoint several of the communist bases in Cambodia. We're going to take one out. Show the sons of bitches that we know how to fight the war even if no one will let us do it."

"Maybe I was wrong about this," said Anderson. "There might be good reasons for those camps not to be hit."

"If there was a secret mission or reason," said Sadler, "I'd know about it. I know we have to be careful that we don't step on anyone's toes, but there is nothing going on around any of those camps."

"Maybe something directed from the Pentagon," said Anderson.

"That's why I took the job of assistant operations officer. If there was something going on, they'd have to alert us so that we didn't screw it up. There is nothing."

"Maybe these SEALs you talked about are doing something."

Sadler pulled up in front of the rearm point. There was another jeep sitting there. It had the company's insignia painted on the rear bumper.

"The others are here," said Sadler as he turned off the ignition.

"What about the SEALs?" asked Anderson again.

"There is no one operating around any of our possible targets. I've checked everything very carefully."

Anderson followed Sadler into the rearm bunker. There was a string of bare light bulbs hanging from a beam that ran the length of the bunker. There were boxes of ammo, crates of it and cans of it. It was arranged according to type of weapon, with the 7.62-mm ammo for the M-60 machine guns closest to the door. There was also M-16 ammo and pistol ammo. Next to that were the racks where the 2.75-inch rockets were stored. Anderson stopped in his tracks when he recognized DeWeiss sitting there, a file in one hand and a rocket propped against his leg.

"What in the hell are you doing?" he asked.

"Filing the numbers off the rocket," said DeWeiss.

"I mean why are you here? You tried to talk me out of this thing."

"And I would again. I didn't want you jumping into something that you didn't understand."

"But I do understand."

DeWeiss nodded and set aside the rocket and his file. "But you're not here because you want to be one of the guys. You're not here to support your buddies in their crazy mission. You're here because this is something that you want to do."

"I guess I'd have to agree with that," said Anderson. "Now what can I do?"

Sadler picked up a file and handed it to Anderson. "Okay, we want to remove all obvious markings. Everything that can lead back here. All serial numbers stamped into the metal. Everything."

"How far down do I have to file?"

Sadler shrugged. "That's a good question. I know the FBI had some techniques that can bring out the serial numbers filed off guns, but it's a destructive process. I doubt that the North Vietnamese would have the technology to do it. Just file away until you can't read it any more."

"How many rockets?"

"Fourteen pairs. We're taking two gunships with the M-21 armament system."

"Which is?" asked Anderson. As a slick pilot, he hadn't learned the jargon for the various gunship weapon packages.

"That contains the XM-134 miniguns and the XM-158 2.75-inch rocket launchers. Fourteen rockets fired as seven pairs."

"So what's the plan?"

"Lead ship carries two pair of smoke rockets to mark the target. Second ship hits it with fourteen rockets as the first comes around to launch the last rockets. Then we hose down the camp with miniguns and M-60s, finally breaking away and running for home."

Anderson shook his head. "I can't see us doing much damage to them. If they've got a bunker and tunnel system like they have in South Vietnam, they'll just crawl into that and we'll be fucked."

"Except," said Sadler, "the intelligence reports say that they have some above-ground bunkers, but not an extensive system. They don't fear an attack in Cambodia."

"Then we'll be forcing them to create the system so that if our people ever go in, they'll have to dig them out."

"I don't think so," said Sadler. "Oh, at first there'll be some activity, but when there are no follow-up raids, they'll stop digging. We'll have caused them a lot of extra work and denied them supplies."

"But more importantly," said DeWeiss, "we'll get them thinking. What if it wasn't a one-time raid? They'll be waiting for the other shoe to drop."

"Then this is more psychological than destructive."

Again Sadler shrugged. He sat down on an upturned ammo crate and said, "I suppose so. But it gives us a chance to get even for the last couple of days."

"Too bad we can't get some kind of access to assess the damage we've done."

"That may be the best part of the plan," said Sadler. "Once we go in, the Green Berets or the SEALs or an LRRP team will follow to look over the damage."

"You arranged that?" Anderson couldn't believe it.

"No. No. You misunderstand. It's a natural mission. Reports come out that one of the camps has been hit. Someone will go in to look at the damage and, by watching the intel reports, we'll find out just how we did."

"Just how are you going to get the ships out of the revetments?"

Sadler held up a hand and said, "We'll have a complete

briefing tomorrow. Tonight we've got to finish the work here. I'll take care of all the other problems."

Anderson looked at the rocket, turning it around.

"Careful or you'll damage the fins."

"Yeah," said Anderson. He studied the rocket and then the interior of the bunker. There was a dirty smell in the air— too much dust from too many feet tracking in mud. The light wasn't as good as it could have been, and then Anderson wondered how safe it was to be sitting there with explosives all around. It seemed that the place could blow up at any moment.

Sadler stood and came closer. He crouched and pointed. "You need to file off the numbers there and there."

"What about the insignia?"

"Hell, they're going to know it was Americans. We just don't want them to know which Americans."

They worked in silence. The only sound coming from inside the bunker was the quiet rasp of the file against the metal of the rockets. Outside there was the constant sound of helicopters on the airfield, and an occasional detonation from the 105-mm howitzer battery as its guns fired marking rounds.

Sadler circulated periodically, looking at the rockets, making sure Anderson and DeWeiss had filed deeply enough. Satisfied, he returned to his own work.

It didn't take them long to finish. Sadler inspected all the rockets again and then told the men to stack them at the rear, where they would be out of sight. During the day, gun teams from Cu Chi, Tay Ninh, and a dozen other places might use the rearm point, and Sadler wanted to make sure that no one would take the special ones accidentally.

Finished, they cleaned up, put everything away, and then turned off the lights. They walked to the jeeps outside, and Sadler said, "I'll buy everyone a beer over at the club."

"A beer would be good," said Anderson.

"And no one says a word about this. Tomorrow, I'll take

care of the scheduling details. You all be ready to go about dusk."

"Got it," said DeWeiss.

As the first jeep roared off, Anderson looked at Sadler and asked, "You sure this is a good idea?"

"You want out, just say the word and you're out. I'll find another pilot."

"No," said Anderson. "I'm in."

Sadler climbed behind the wheel and started the engine. "Then I'll buy you the beer."

In the club, they found a table to themselves, and Sadler bought a beer for each of them. They sat there drinking quietly, while the music on the jukebox told them that this could be the last time. The Rolling Stones song had a way of predicting things. Someone had played it over and over the night before the flight had gotten shot to hell.

They drank in silence. It was like the night before the big invasion. Everyone knew that the next day a large number of them would be dead, and everyone knew that it wouldn't be him. It would be one of the others.

Sadler leaned forward, looking like he wanted to say something, and then sat back. The wicker creaked with his movements.

The song ended and some one started feeding coins into the slot machine that accepted them one at a time but returned almost nothing. Not like the slots in Las Vegas that paid off 97 percent of the time.

"Tomorrow," said DeWeiss, holding his beer can high.

Anderson shrugged and tapped his can against DeWeiss's. The others did the same and they all drank.

Brown shouldered his way through the crowd and said, "I've been looking for you, Anderson. You missed the ACs meeting this evening. If you plan on staying a PPIC you've got to be more responsible than that."

"That was my fault, Captain," said Sadler. "Mister Anderson came down to ask about enemy weapons capability in our AO and I kept him there reading about everything up to and including 37-millimeter."

"There's no 37-millimeter around here," said Brown.

"There have been no reports for the last month, but before that a couple of units ran into some. The major threat is the .51-cal, but since he asked, I gave him the whole range of weapons."

"What'd you learn?" asked Brown.

"That the .51-cal is the same as the 12.7 and that they can shoot your ass out of the sky up to about eleven thousand feet," said Anderson.

"Right," said Brown. "Most impressive. Tomorrow I want you at the ACs meeting without fail." Brown turned and left.

"That might cause us a problem," said Anderson.

"I doubt it," said DeWeiss. "You notice that he didn't mention my absence?"

"So?"

"So, tomorrow you'll be with me, taking care of some bit of business. Since I'm the unit IP, he won't question me about your absence."

"Maybe it'd be better if I didn't go along," said Anderson. He took a swig from his beer and set it on the table.

"No," said Sadler. "We have everything ready now, and I have the latest intel reports. We go tomorrow."

The jukebox began another song finally. The man who had been playing the slot machine gave up on it and started feeding the coins into the juke. He announced that he wanted some return on his investment.

"When the flight is released tomorrow," said Sadler, "we meet in my office in the operations bunker. We'll look at the maps then and have the final briefing."

"I've a few general questions," said Anderson.

"Tomorrow. I've worked this thing out carefully, so you'll get everything you need then."

"How are we going to cover our trail?" asked Anderson anyway.

Sadler laughed and shook his head. "That's the easiest

part. No one pays any attention to helicopters operating on the field. Fox never goes out to count them and the tower assumes that anyone getting into one has the authorization to fly it. We could steal the flight and no one would try to stop us. We just fly away, do our thing, and come back. No problem at all."

"It seems like it's going to be too easy to do this," said Anderson.

"We can make it harder if you'd like," said Sadler. He glanced around, looking at the other men in the club. "But why should we?"

"Why should we?" echoed Anderson.

Sadler slid back and stood up. "Then tomorrow, gentlemen. We'll teach Mister Charles a lesson."

They got up and left the club without a word to any of the others.

ELEVEN

ANDERSON was nervous the whole next day. He was worried from the moment that he had been awakened, and the feeling had not deserted him at any time. He flew the first lift and then the second and finally the third, while the Peter Pilot just sat there, playing with the radios and watching the war pass him by. Anderson didn't trust the man with the controls.

And he was sure that he was going to die. The aircraft was going to fall apart in midair, or the enemy was going to be waiting in ambush, as they had a few days earlier. Anderson knew that his luck couldn't run good in two such fights, but the enemy wasn't around. The third lift had taken some fire, but the LZ couldn't be called hot. It was more like lukewarm. The grunts had opened up, killing two VC, and that had been the end of the trouble.

At lunch, back at Cu Chi, Anderson found that he wasn't hungry. Many times before, as he moved through the chow line, he had realized that he wasn't hungry, but most of that had been from seeing what was being served. This time it was nerves. It was the knowledge that he was going to fly into Cambodia.

Only a few times had the flight ventured close to Cambodia, and each time they had been warned about the defenses set up there. The charts and maps were marked with warnings that said "Overflight Requires Diplomatic Clearance." The Ho Chi Minh Trail was not far on the other side of the border.

Anderson ignored his food and drank huge quantities of Kool-Aid. The last thing he wanted was to be dehydrated for the upcoming mission. He was sweating heavily, more than the unpleasant humidity of the day demanded. Halfway through the meal he got up to go the bathroom, and twenty minutes later he went again. It wasn't because of the Kool-Aid.

After lunch, with no call for the flight crews to return to the aircraft, Anderson wandered the company area, stepping into one hootch after another. He couldn't sit still and didn't get involved in any conversations. He wandered around because he couldn't sit still.

In the movies, the men going into battle were calm. They knew what was coming and what they had to do. They gambled and read and wrote letters, but Anderson couldn't do any of that. The energy was bubbling through him, making it impossible for him to sit quietly. For a moment he had considered writing to Susan, but she hadn't bothered to write since the first letter. Then he thought about Rachel, a lovely women who deserved to be told something about how he had died, if he did—but again, he couldn't sit still long enough to write her.

He reached the end of the area and stood staring into the bright afternoon sunlight. It was so bright that it seemed hazy and, even with his sunglasses, it was hard to see. Aircraft hovered around on the end of the runway, and the heat rising from it gave the airfield an unreal quality. And then there was the smell. JP-4. That very odor in coming years would, he thought, be enough to conjure up this vision—the white-hot look of the airfield at midday, with a half-dozen helicopters hovering around it like overgrown insects.

He turned and walked back through the company area, suddenly at peace with himself. Something had come to him in those few moments, and he felt better. Suddenly he was like the sleeping soldiers on the invasion ships: calm and at peace.

The flight was called out and Anderson let the pilot handle some of the flying duties, relaxing while AFVN filled his earphones with the latest rock music (which in Vietnam was about six months out of phase with the rest of the world).

They picked up the grunts, who had failed to find the enemy, which no longer surprised Anderson. If they were interested in finding the VC, then they had to make the search at night, when the VC moved. It was so much easier to look in the daylight, however. You didn't have to be a great soldier to survive in the daylight. It was one more indication of the route-step approach to the war.

And then the flight was released. They flew back to Cu Chi, refueled and rearmed, and landed in the revetments. Anderson filled out the book while the pilot copied down the information that the accountants in operations would want—number of passengers carried, number of sorties flown, number of rounds expended.

As he walked across the road, Anderson saw DeWeiss disappear into the operations bunker. Anderson changed course and entered behind the other man. He followed him downstairs and around to the back.

Sadler sat behind his desk, and seated in front of him was the gun-team platoon leader. Anderson's first thought was that something had gone wrong, but Sadler waved him forward. He then understood why the fourth man hadn't been in the bunker the night before. Captain Wilde had to maintain a low profile so that no one asked a lot of hard questions.

"Final briefing now."

"I was wondering about this," said Anderson. "I didn't know who was going to fire the guns, because I have so little experience at it."

"Captain Wilde will be team leader and will mark the target on the first pass. Anderson, you and I will be in the second ship and make the first firing pass. You'll be flying and I'll use the weapons systems."

Sadler stood up then and moved around to the counter and said, "I don't want anyone back here for the next thirty minutes."

"Yes, sir," said the clerk.

Sadler then pushed one of the work tables across the entrance. He returned and sat down.

"Captain Wilde will do the navigation. We fly at fifteen hundred feet to Tay Ninh, south of the city and the base, and then drop to low level. From that point we never climb above five hundred feet until we make the runs."

Wilde turned and said, "Anderson, one thing you'll need to know is to not overfly the target. You break the run short and turn out."

"Yes, sir."

DeWeiss said, "Sadler should call the break for you."

Sadler pulled out a map and then said, "Okay, our target is the training and resupply facility north of Savy Rieng." He turned and opened the safe that was behind him, pulling out an aerial photograph. "This is the only picture I have of the target."

Anderson took it and could see nothing other than the trees, a stream that cut through them, and a small dirt road. Then, staring at it, he saw what looked like part of a building. He nodded as he began to see the outlines of the camp. It was like one of those puzzles with all the objects hidden in the picture.

He handed the photo to DeWeiss, who gave it to Wilde. Once they had all seen it, Sadler went back to the map. He briefed them on the approaches and the suspected antiaircraft emplacements along the border.

"Low-level, we should avoid all those. Once we're across the border, every asshole with an AK is going to take pot-shots at us if he can. We'll have to ignore that to concentrate on the target."

Wilde took over, giving them the most likely directions for the gun runs, explaining that they would gradually shift them around so that they weren't overflying the same route each time. The door guns would be responsible for covering them on the breaks if they didn't get the daisy chain set up right.

After Wilde had given his portion of the briefing, Sadler said, "If you're shot down, you'll have to escape and evade to the east, into South Vietnam. If you try to get a rescue ship into Cambodia, we'll have a lot of explaining to do. Under ideal circumstances, it'll take only a few hours to get out of Cambodia and get help. If you can't move, then call for a rescue and we'll think of something."

"That's providing that the other ship can't provide assistance," said DeWeiss.

"What about refueling?" asked Anderson.

"Shit, we can use the facilities at Tay Ninh if we need them. If not, we refuel and rearm here."

Anderson took another look at the maps and then said, "Anyone check the weather?"

"Weather is going to be the least of our problems. Anything else?"

"You said something about the door gunners."

Wilde spoke up. "I think I did, but you don't have to worry about them. They're my people and know what they're doing."

"Then why didn't you get all gun pilots to go on this thing?" asked Anderson.

"Because it's strictly voluntary. We let hints drop and take who we can get."

"All right," said Sadler, "we meet at the aircraft at nineteen hundred tonight. Let's not have a parade out there. One at a time."

Wilde stood then. "I'll leave first."

"Go ahead," said Sadler. "See you tonight."

When the gun-team platoon leader was gone, Anderson asked, "How're we going to explain any new holes in the aircraft?"

"That's simple. We're not."

Anderson avoided everyone for the next two hours. He stayed in his hootch, leaving only to use the latrine. When he could stand it no more, he picked up his chicken plate, pistol, and helmet so that he could go out to the aircraft. As he did, he wondered why he hadn't thought of leaving everything on the flight line, or in operations. That was the thing he should do.

He walked out the back door of his hootch and saw no one around. He cut across the company area, behind the enlisted men's club, and then through their area. No one appeared to ask him where he was going with his gear. He hurried across the road and disappeared among the revetments. Now it would be difficult for anyone to see him.

On the flight line, he could see no one else. He walked over to the helicopter he had flown that day and climbed into the cargo compartment. For twenty minutes he sat there, listening to the constant noise from the airfield. It wasn't as hot as it had been and, for the first time in days, he felt comfortable—no sweat dripping. He leaned against the gray soundproofing of the cargo compartment and stared out the windshield at the bright lights on one of the hangars. Men were working on a helicopter, its rotors missing. A yellow scaffolding was erected on the aircraft's side, and two huge lights were shining down on the engine deck. It was a great target for the enemy, if there had been any high ground around from which to launch rockets or fire mortars.

Finally, he saw DeWeiss cross the road and head toward the other end of the flight line, where the C-model gunships were parked. Anderson picked up his gear, dropped to the ground, and hurried in that direction.

DeWeiss saw him coming and raised a hand in greeting. Not far behind was Sadler. As he approached, he asked, "Anyone seen Wilde?"

"Not yet," said Anderson.

"Okay, we've got aircraft zero two seven and six one two. Let's get a preflight done." He turned to DeWeiss. "You know how to preflight the weapons systems?"

"I can handle it."

"Then let's do it."

Sadler and Anderson went over to six one two. Sadler threw his gear into the cargo compartment and said, "You know the hydraulics systems on these are different than the Ds and Hs that we normally fly. You lose hydraulic pressure and you've about ten minutes to put it down. After that you won't be able to move the controls."

"I know that," said Anderson.

"Just wanted you aware of it so that you'll keep an eye on the hydraulic pressure."

"Got it."

Anderson took care of the external preflight, ignoring the guns and the rocket pods. Sadler checked them over, along with the sights and radios inside. As they finished, Wilde and the door gunners appeared.

"Sorry about that," he said, "but Fox caught me and wanted to talk for a minute. Couldn't get rid of him."

"Preflights have been taken care of," said Sadler.

"Okay, then let's crank and fly over to rearm for those rockets that you doctored."

Wilde headed over to the other aircraft and Sadler climbed into the right seat. Anderson took the left. As he buckled himself in, Sadler said, "You do the run-up."

Anderson nodded and put on his helmet. He then followed the laminated card to start the engine. Once that was accomplished, he checked all the gauges and then used the intercom. "We're ready."

Sadler reached down and changed the frequency on the

Fox Mike. He then used the floor button for the radio. "Revenge One, this is Revenge Two."

"Go."

"Ready for takeoff."

"Two is ready."

Sadler turned his selector switch to the UHF and called the tower, requesting permission for a flight of two to go from the revetments to the rearm point.

"Roger, six one two, you are cleared for departure."

"Six one two on the go."

Sadler took the controls, picked up to a hover, and then slipped right, out of the revetment. He hovered between two others and then turned so that he was next to the runway. When he was joined by the second aircraft, he took off, climbing out to the south. They flew around the traffic pattern, landing at the rearm point.

As they touched down, Sadler said, "You've got it."

Anderson responded. "I've got it."

"You sit here while we get the rockets changed. You get any kind of radio transmission to us, you say nothing. You tell me about it and I'll handle it."

"Got it."

Anderson sat there and watched as the crew chief and gunner began to unload the rockets that were already in the tubes. They carried them into the bunkers. Sadler and Wilde helped, and in a few minutes they had the tubes empty. A moment later, they began loading them again. With that finished, both door gunners brought out more M-60 ammo for use in the miniguns and the M-60s. One of them carried out a box of grenades. Finally they brought out bandoliers of ammo for the M-16s that would be carried in the rear of the helicopters. The theory was that if they got shot down, the crew chief and gunner would use the M-60s and the pilots would use the M-16s. Each of them had a pistol and a survival knife.

They finished quickly, and Sadler climbed into the cockpit. He put on his helmet and keyed the mike. "We're ready."

There was a breathless quality to his voice, as if he had run a long way. It was the first time that Anderson had heard anything over the radio or intercom that suggested anyone had emotions. Everyone was so careful to sound calm and reserved. No one wanted anyone else to think that they were excited or scared.

"Okay," said Sadler. "Why don't you fly for a while and get the feel of the aircraft."

"I've got it," said Anderson.

As he watched, the other aircraft came to a low hover because of all the weight from the weapons and ammo and fuel. They lined up on the open field outside the rearm point, the aircraft light on the skids because neither could maintain a hover. Gun lead began to slide forward, making a running takeoff. Anderson followed, first getting light on the skids and then kicking the pedals to break free from the ground. He slid forward, gaining speed until he was able to get up two or three feet, mostly through ground effect—the rotorwash, sucked through the rotor system, was creating a cushion of air, holding the aircraft just off the ground.

As he gained speed, they went through transition, leaving the rotorwash behind them. He eased the cyclic to the rear, using their forward motion to help create lift, just as an airplane used the wind over the wings to help it fly.

Anderson closed on the lead aircraft and, as he did, Wilde rolled over, increasing their speed to one hundred twenty knots. The slicks normally cruised at eighty, but the C-model, with a heavy-duty rotor system, was designed for higher speeds.

They followed Highway One south, skirting Trang Bang and Go Dau Ha before heading northwest. After what seemed only a few minutes, Anderson saw the faint glow of light that marked Tay Ninh city. As they approached it, he suddenly realized exactly what they were doing—violating rules and regulations and international law. It wasn't like the high-school pranks where the police slapped a few wrists if anyone was caught, and everyone had a good laugh when it was over. This was something much more serious and more dangerous. People were about to die.

He kept his eyes moving, from the instrument panel, to the aircraft ahead of him, to the scene on the ground, a dark scene with only occasional lights. He was lost in a dark cocoon where no one could talk to him if he decided he didn't want to hear anything.

He glanced at Sadler, who was leaning forward against the restraining harness, his hands on his knees. He looked like a man who was hard of hearing, leaning toward his boss at a board meeting. He raised a gloved hand and wiped his face, pushing the boom mike out of the way. He readjusted it, touching it to his lips.

There was no way out now. Anderson knew he couldn't just decide that they were wrong and ask to turn around. They were committed to the mission unless something happened. If they lost hydraulic power, or the chip detector went off, then they would have a reason for turning back. If not, then he was committed.

"Beginning a descent," said Wilde.

"Roger," said Anderson. The move to squeeze the trigger for the mike was a reflex, the answer, automatic. He lowered the collective and eased up on the cyclic, adding a little pedal. As he did, he reached up and turned off the rotating beacon. There was no reason to advertise their presence now. They wouldn't run into other blacked-out aircraft, because no one would be running without lights. Except them.

They leveled off about fifty feet above the ground. It was black now. There was a gray line in the distance that was the horizon. There were clumps of black that reached up into the charcoal of the night sky. They slowed then and climbed slightly, away from the last of the obstacles on the ground. Now, at a hundred feet, they skimmed along, avoiding the villages and hamlets and hiding places of the Vietcong.

"We're about to cross the border," said Sadler on the intercom.

Anderson felt his grip tighten on the cyclic. His nerves were suddenly rubbed raw. His fingers ached with the strain and he consciously relaxed them. He rolled his shoulders and swiveled his head. The tension didn't go away now.

Off to the right, in the distance, a string of glowing green tracers flashed into the sky—someone firing a weapon at something. There was no answering fire.

"That's it," said Sadler. "We're in Cambodia."

Over the radio came: "Descending. Lights on dim flash. Do you have me in sight?"

"Roger," said Anderson.

"Close it up now."

Anderson added a little power and drew nearer to the lead ship. He felt the tension in his belly as he began to sweat. He felt it on his sides, under his arms, and dripping from his forehead. He wanted to turn the controls over to Sadler, but the other man was using the map lights to read the chart held in his hand. He was checking the navigation of the lead ship.

"We're getting close," said Sadler.

Anderson didn't respond. He kept looking at the instruments, now glowing a dim red in the lights that weren't supposed to destroy night vision. They had turned them so low that he could barely see the needles. It seemed that everything was in the green. Fuel looked good. Airspeed was low, but he didn't mind that.

"Get ready," said Sadler.

Anderson felt his stomach tumble and his heart climb into his throat. He hadn't been so scared since the night flight when he'd gotten vertigo and thought he was going to fly into the ground. His heart was hammering and his breathing was rapid. All his muscles hurt now, from the strain of trying to fly the aircraft. He wanted out, wanted to land and run from the helicopter, but he couldn't. He couldn't turn and flee, but had to go forward into this.

"We're about five out," said Wilde on the radio.

"Roger." Anderson choked the word out. It seemed to stick in his throat.

"You okay?" asked Sadler.

"Fine."

"Second thoughts?"

"Second and third," said Anderson.

"That's it," said Wilde. "Target in sight.

"Oh, Christ," said Anderson on the intercom. "Here we go for real." He dumped the nose as Wilde began heading into the target. "This is it," he said.

TWELVE

T HE first rockets lit up the sky and the ground in a white-hot explosion of flying debris. In the flash of the fireball and then the burning of the hootches, Anderson could see men running, many of them armed.

"Breaking right," came the call from Wilde.

"Rolling in."

Anderson aimed the nose of his aircraft at the center of the fires that now were burning. He dived at it as Sadler took the sight, maneuvering it on his side of the cockpit. Anderson felt the aircraft shudder, and there were flashes of brightness as Sadler fired the rockets. Anderson watched their flaming motors as the rockets rived into the center of the camp.

"Break! Break!"

Anderson realized that he was staring at the target, diving down into it. He pulled the collective and pushed the cyclic to the right stop. The nose pitched up and they began a turning climb. Behind him the machine guns began to hammer as the chief and door gun opened fire.

He came around again. Out the right door he saw Wilde and DeWeiss start their second run. Rockets rippled, trailing fire. Orange flame flashed as they dived into the camp and ignited.

Now firing broke out below them, strobing flashes as the enemy shot back. Streams of green and white tracers came at them. Anderson felt some of the rounds slamming into the aircraft, but the instruments stayed in the green.

He lined up, the nose of his aircraft pointing into the camp. He could see the enemy down there. Some were running around. Others were crouching, kneeling, their weapons pointed up, firing. Flickering lights marked the enemy soldiers.

Sadler fired the rockets, letting the last of the seven pair go. There were more explosions below and fire was spreading everywhere. There were secondary detonations as the enemy's ammo blew up. A fireball burst upward, a great rolling column of orange and yellow and black that climbed higher.

The hammering in the back of the helicopter never ceased. Anderson saw the lines of ruby-red tracers slashing downward, striking the ground and then tumbling. More tracers, green and white, came at him, first looking like baseballs and then watermelons as the enemy found the range.

Anderson broke to the right again, but not climbing as he had the first time. He stayed close to the trees and then jerked back on the cyclic, trying to fool the enemy gunners.

Wilde rolled in with his miniguns firing on both sides. The muzzle flash looked like a continuous spear of fire lancing outward nearly five feet. The tracers looked like a giant red ray from a Martian death weapon raking the ground. In the flaming wreckage of the camp, Anderson saw the enemy soldiers dying as the ray struck out to touch them.

As the lead ship broke to the right, Anderson rolled in

again, covering it. Sadler was firing their miniguns. The hammering of the M-60s was lost in the buzz-saw sound of the miniguns. They ripped and tore the ground, and men tumbled and rolled and died. The firing from the ground seemed to decrease as the men there scrambled for safety.

Now the door gunner was throwing grenades as fast as he could pull the pins. He was emptying the rear of the aircraft, and there was a series of explosions below as the grenades detonated.

Anderson broke and lead rolled in for a final pass. The miniguns were firing again, shredding everything in their path. More fires were started by the tracers. The flickering, flashing, strobing light gave the ground an unreal look, like an old movie shown at too slow a speed. There were impressions of men falling, but the bodies disappeared in the darkness.

Anderson came around for his final run. Below him there were lumps lying on the ground, scattered black lumps that were the bodies of the dead and the dying. Few men were now shooting into the sky. The crew chief stepped to the skid, the M-60 on a bungee cord pointed to the front. He was leaning over the whirling barrels of the miniguns, trying to avoid the flame shooting out as he aimed at men to the side.

Anderson extended the gun run. He flew down toward the enemy camp, the guns blazing as the bullets slammed into the ground and the hootches and the men. He saw the men fall. He saw them throw their weapons down and try to run. They were caught in the back and smashed to the ground. There were explosions all around him. Flaming debris leaped into the air as supplies detonated and destroyed themselves.

The camp was on fire, the flames shooting fifty, a hundred feet in the air. There were explosions ripping through it as the fires raged. Men were silhouetted against the flames, running, scrambling, and then falling. A hundred bodies, maybe more, were scattered in the center of the camp. The firing, which had been intense, had now almost completely died. A few weapons fired, their tracers arcing into the night, but not close to either of the helicopters.

"Final run," said Wilde.

Anderson broke to the right and began his climb out.

Now the lead gunship rolled in, but the miniguns were quiet. Both the crew chief and the gunner were firing the M-60s, and one of the pilots was shooting his M-16 out the window.

Then, in the jungle to the north of the camp, a huge weapon began to hammer. Four strings of tracers came upward out of the darkness as a Quad-50 tried to knock down the helicopter.

"Quad-50," shouted Wilde, stunned. "Breaking right."

As it began to fire, and Wilde broke away, Anderson dived in to cover him. Both miniguns opened up, the tracers digging into the darkness around the Quad-50. Ruby-red tracers disappeared into the trees that protected the enemy weapon.

The enemy didn't care that Anderson was attacking. He kept his sights on the lead aircraft. The emerald tracers reached out and touched the helicopter. It jerked right, then left, and then dived, trying to get away from the enemy.

Anderson passed over the camp, violating that rule. He dived toward the Quad-50, trying to destroy it. Sadler was squeezing off short bursts from the miniguns. There was a second of total sound and fire, and then silence. Then more shooting.

"Taking hits," said Wilde, his voice normal.

There was a flash of flame on top of the helicopter and then darkness.

"Losing oil pressure. I'm running for it."

"Roger," said Anderson. "Breaking left."

He turned in the opposite direction, diving for the ground. The Quad-50 fell silent, and Anderson didn't now if they had gotten it, or if its targets had disappeared.

Anderson looped around the burning camp. Flames were

shooting higher into the night sky. There were vehicles burning now, and there were still explosions that mushroomed sparks and flames skyward. All the enemy gunners had fallen silent.

Anderson hugged the ground. He was breathing heavily, but since the attack had started he'd been too busy to be scared. He'd flown the aircraft, doing just what he'd been taught to do without thinking about it.

"You want me to take over?" asked Sadler.

"I've got it," said Anderson.

"Try to get around to where lead is," said Sadler.

"That's what I'm trying to do."

On the radio, Sadler said, "Revenge Two, this is One. Say status."

"We're in trouble," said Wilde, his voice now icy. "Multiple hits. I think we're going down."

"Say location."

"Running for the border, but I don't think we'll make it."

"Roger," said Sadler. "Can you give us some light to find you?"

"Rotating beacon on," said Wilde.

Sadler slapped Anderson on the shoulder and pointed with a gloved hand. "There."

"Got him."

"We have you in sight," said Sadler on the radio. As he spoke, the beacon went out.

"He crash?" asked Anderson.

"No. No sense in advertising his whereabouts to the enemy. They might be looking for him."

Anderson turned toward the lead helicopter.

"Revenge One, we're now on the ground."

"Roger. You have wounded?"

"That's a negative. Everyone is healthy."

"Roger. We're inbound your location. Can you help us find you?"

"Roger."

Anderson climbed slightly. He glanced over his shoulder,

through the cargo compartment door. The fires in the enemy camp lit the area like a beacon. They should be visible well into South Vietnam. There were probably Americans in South Vietnam who could see the fire. If they could figure out that it was an enemy camp burning they would probably be cheering.

"Do you have us?" asked Wilde.

"Negative."

They expected a response, but there was silence at the other end. Sadler keyed the mike. "Revenge Two."

There was no answer, and Sadler asked, "What in the hell could have happened to them?"

Anderson leveled off and began a gentle turn to the left so that Sadler would have the best view of the ground. He wondered if they had gotten back into South Vietnam yet or if they were still on the wrong side of the border.

"Revenge Two, say status." Sadler turned in his seat and pointed at the crew chief and gunner. "Either of you see anything back there?"

"Negative sir. Just the enemy camp burning like a son of a bitch."

Anderson completed one orbit and straightened out. He thought about climbing to a higher altitude, but if they were still in Cambodia, it would just make them a better target.

"We can't leave them," said Sadler.

"We've used about half our fuel."

"We can refuel at Tay Ninh, which can't be more than twenty, thirty minutes away."

Then, suddenly: "Revenge One, this is Two."

"Go, two."

"Had a couple of minor problems. Do you have us in sight?"

"That's a negative."

"Roger. Be advised that we have turned on the rotating beacon and are on the ground."

Sadler twisted in his seat, looking to the left, then out the front. He turned and tried to look out the right. "Anyone see anything?"

"There! On the ground to our seven o'clock," said the crew chief.

Anderson banked around in a quick turn that forced everyone down in the seats.

"Got a beacon," said Sadler on the radio. As he spoke the beacon went out.

"That's us."

"We're inbound your location."

"Roger."

Anderson began a descent, his eyes fixed on the site where the beacon had flashed. It looked to be fairly open, although there were trees and jungle all around it. Now that he was heading back toward the enemy camp, he could see the fires there better—huge fires that lit the night sky. There were flashes from it as the last of the ammo stocks exploded.

"We need to bear to the right," said Sadler.

Anderson turned, and heard a quiet ripping sound to his right.

"We're taking fire from the ground," said the door gunner.

"Well, return it," shouted the crew chief.

"No!" ordered Sadler. "It wasn't close. Let's not mark our position for the enemy."

A stream of green tracers climbed into the night in front of the helicopter. Anderson didn't know how far away they were, but he didn't hear the weapon firing.

"We hear you," said Wilde. "Be advised there are enemy soldiers around us."

"Do they have you located?"

"Negative."

More firing broke out below, but the rounds flashed by harmlessly. Green and white tracers ripped at the sky. Muzzles flashed on the ground.

"Revenge Two, we need some help locating you."

"Roger."

Anderson saw the beacon flash once and then go out. He

turned toward it and, as he did, it seemed that the jungle was alive with enemy soldiers. Weapons opened up, sparkling in the night like the fireflies of a hot, lazy evening. A few rounds struck the side of the aircraft.

Now Anderson was calm. He didn't think about the bullets coming at him and tried not to see the tracers. He ignored them, watching the ground for a sign of the downed helicopter. He thought he'd found it, shallowed his approach.

On the radio, Wilde said, "We've got you in sight. Turn about ten degrees to the south."

Anderson made the correction and lowered the collective. He spotted the black shape of the downed helicopter sitting on the dark gray of the ground. He dropped the nose for speed.

"Sir, we've got enemy soldiers all around us."

"Don't fire yet," said Sadler.

Anderson flared then, bringing the nose up, He lost sight of the downed ship. He sucked in a little pitch to help slow the aircraft, leveled the skids, and dropped to the ground. As he did, three men loomed out of the darkness, running at them. The door gunner swung his weapon on them, but saw that they were Americans.

DeWeiss leaped into the cargo compartment, crouched behind Anderson's seat, and slapped him on the shoulder. "Nicely done. Put yourself in for a medal from petty cash."

Wilde was slower. He stood with his back to them and opened fire with an M-16, putting holes in the sides and belly of the downed helicopter so that the JP-4 bled onto the crash site. When the weapon was empty, he turned and ran for Anderson's ship.

Around them it seemed that the jungle had come alive. There were flashes of light and movement—quick, jerky movement—all around.

"I think we've been spotted."

Anderson started to suck in some pitch. The aircraft rose, light on the skids. There was a roaring in his head, but not from the turbine. His blood was pounding. He wanted to get out. Each second on the ground was one more that the enemy had to aim and shoot at him. The back of his neck itched, as if he could feel the enemy rifle sights pinned there. It would be an almost impossible shot for an enemy gunner, given the helmet and the armored seat, but that didn't make the feeling go away.

"Come on," he grumbled to himself. "Come on."

Wilde looped across the open ground, but stopped short of the aircraft. He spun and pulled the pin on a smoke grenade. As he tossed it at the downed ship, he leaped into the cargo compartment.

"Go! Go! *Go!*"

Anderson shoved the cyclic forward as he sucked in an arm-load of pitch. The aircraft leaped almost straight up as the nose fell, and then raced for the tree line. As it did, the jungle erupted into fire as the enemy opened up, trying to bring them down.

There was a brilliant flash of fire and light behind them as the downed aircraft exploded. The smoke grenade had set the JP-4 on fire. The fuel cells then blew up.

Both the door gunner and the crew chief opened up with their M-60s. Sadler tried to use the sight for the miniguns, but was having trouble. Anderson climbed enough to get over the trees and then skimmed along them.

"Climb!" yelled Sadler.

But Anderson didn't. He turned to the south, looping around. The sky was bright with the enemy tracers searching for them. The fire lit the crash site. They could see men running around it now, trying to get to the aircraft. Sadler didn't wait. He opened up, raking the area with the last of the ammo from the miniguns. The enemy soldiers scattered, two dozen of them falling under the hail of lead.

Anderson broke away from the LZ, and began a slow climb out. There was firing far to the rear of them—from the sound alone, hundreds of enemy soldiers trying to down them. No one had them spotted now.

From the rear, someone was shouting, "Go, baby, go!"

Anderson leveled out. In the distance, in front of them, was the faint glow of Tay Ninh. In the World, a city the size of Tay Ninh would have been a huge, bright beacon beckoning them. Here it was barely bright enough for them to see.

"That's it," shouted Sadler. "We've crossed the border. We're in South Vietnam."

Everyone heard him. Cheering erupted in the back of the aircraft. The men were screaming and applauding and laughing. Anderson felt himself relax. His fingers unclamped from the controls, taking on the loose-fingered grip that was supposed to be the way to do it. Suddenly he felt the aches and pains of the strain. But he didn't care. He felt the laughter bubbling through him.

"All right!" he screamed. "All right!"

On the intercom, Sadler said, "I've got it."

And Anderson said, "You've fucking well got it." He took his hands from the controls and seemed to collapse into his seat. Using the floor mike button he said, "We did it!"

"We fucking did!" said Sadler.

Anderson striped off his helmet and looked into the cargo compartment. It was jammed with the six men and the equipment, but no one looked uncomfortable. They were laughing and joking and hitting at each other.

"Everyone all right?" asked Anderson.

"We're fucking beautiful," yelled Wilde. "And so are you. Hell of a job."

"That'll give Charlie something to think about."

"Yeah, he won't feel safe in his own bed now. Hot damn! We should have done that before."

Anderson turned and looked out the windshield. They were close to Tay Ninh now. Well inside of South Vietnam. Sadler had climbed to fifteen hundred feet and turned on the beacon and nav lights. Everything on the instrument panel seemed to be intact. The instruments were in the green. Then, in the lower corner of the windshield, Anderson saw a bullet hole. He turned to the right and saw where it had struck the side of the armor seat. Not on the outside, but on the inside, less than an inch from his shoulder and neck.

"Christ!" he said, suddenly feeling cold. It had been that close. And suddenly, he wanted to whoop. To have been that close and gotten away was something that should be celebrated. He put on his helmet and then pointed at the bullet hole.

Sadler glanced at it. "Yeah. Close."

"Too close," said Anderson, but it wasn't. Too close was the one that hit you.

"Okay," said Sadler. "I don't think we should head back to Cu Chi yet."

"Why the hell not?"

"Because this was too good. We've got to go celebrate. I'm heading for the Gunfighter's Club to buy the bar."

"We can't let anyone know what we've done," said Anderson. "It's got to remain a secret."

"Exactly," said Sadler. "So where were we this evening? Well, we bought the bar in Saigon." He glanced at Anderson, his teeth flashing white in his big grin. "An alibi."

"That's fucking beautiful," said Anderson.

"Yeah," said Sadler. "I know. A celebration that provides our alibi, and no one knows what we're celebrating."

"I like it."

"Then the next stop is Saigon."

THIRTEEN

EVEN before they entered the Gunfighter's Club, they could hear the music rocking and the people cheering. A party was in full swing, and it was just the thing that the men needed after the mission. They walked toward the door, and the marshal there nodded at them, seeing the combination of flight suits and jungle fatigues, each with the wings sewn over the left breast.

They hesitated only long enough to secure their pistols in the lockboxes provided, and then opened the doors onto the screaming, cheering, singing, dancing, laughing masses. Two women danced on the stage, neither of them regulars at the club.

Over the noise, Sadler shouted, "Find a table and I'll get the first round."

They worked their way through the mass of humanity and discovered a vacant table in the back. Wilde grabbed a couple of spare chairs from another table and everyone sat down. From their vantage point, they could not see the stage, and that explained why the table was vacant.

Anderson stood for a moment, watching as one of the women unbuttoned her blouse, shedding it and waving it over her head. She wore a white bra that covered her better than most of the bathing suits he'd seen.

He sat down and rubbed his eyes. The smoke was heavy, hanging over them like a thick, blue fog. It burned the eyes and made it hard to breath. It was hot and noisy in the club, but not one of them cared about it.

As they sat there, DeWeiss whooped once and yelled, "God damn that was good."

Sadler arrived with the beers, setting them down in the center of the table. He grabbed one, held it high, and screamed, "To the finest men in the United States Army. Us."

Everyone took a beer, touched them together in a rattling of glass, and then drank. When the toast was complete, Sadler collapsed into a chair.

"I'd like to thank each of you for helping make my dream come true."

"No problem," yelled Wilde. "Our pleasure."

"No," said Sadler, "you deserve thanks. I've been wanting to do this since Tet this year. If Charlie and the NVA can mount a sneak and surprise attack, then I think it's only right that we do the same."

"Regardless of regulations," said Anderson.

"Or in spite of them," said Sadler. "Why should the enemy have all the advantages? I've been here damn near my whole year, and I think I've been on one, maybe two missions, not counting tonight, where it seemed that someone had actually thought the thing through and we accomplished something. The rest of the time we were boring holes in the sky and accomplishing nothing."

"Yeah," said DeWeiss, his head bobbing like those dogs in the rear windows of cars. "We do nothing but run a taxi service that accomplishes less than nothing."

"Except for tonight," said Wilde. "Tonight Charlie felt the sting of air power."

"Finally," said Sadler. "And it was something that we had to do on our own." He sipped his beer and then shook his head. "What in the hell can our so-called leaders be thinking, anyway?"

"I think," said Wilde, "that I can answer that one. There is no drive to get the war over. You come here, as an officer, get your career ticket punched, and then head home covered with glory. You commanded a unit, no matter how small, no matter that it was for six months or less, in combat. A good career move. The best to hope for is a little contact, to have the opportunity to put yourself in for a couple of medals, and then on to the promotion boards. Don't make waves, and get sent home."

"Fuck," said Anderson. "That's no way to win a war."

Wilde rocked back in his chair like he had been struck. "Who in the hell said anything about winning anything? The trick is to get out without having your ass shot off, unless you gain great glory doing it. Our Major Fox might be in some hot water over the boondoogle a couple of days ago, but I doubt it. The losses weren't that bad, and we shot the shit out of a VC company. Lots of enemy dead can make up for a bad mistake."

"Fuck," repeated Anderson.

There was a sudden, wild burst of applause, and the men turned toward the stage. Anderson stood long enough to see that one of the women had thrown away her bra and was attempting to roll her panties down her thighs.

Anderson sat down and asked, "How are we going to explain the loss of the one aircraft?"

"Why should we?" asked Sadler. He grinned, and took a final sip of beer. As he set the empty bottle on the table, he continued. "Suppose that you're, oh, Captain Brown. Now, tomorrow someone comes to you and asks if you happen to know about the helicopter missing from the revetments? What do you say?"

"Which one?"

"Good," said Sadler, nodding. "Or maybe you ask if it's one of the slicks, or say something about knowing nothing about it. The point is, he knows nothing. Now if they come and ask you, what do you say?"

"There's a ship missing?"

"Bravo!" yelled Sadler, sounding as if he was cheering for the naked woman. "We, like everyone else, deny everything. We know nothing about it."

"And how do we explain our absence?"

"If anyone happens to notice," said Sadler, "I was at Battalion talking to a friend there. He'll swear we drank beer there and then I left, coming here."

"And I was working with a couple of men on a gun system that was malfunctioning," said Wilde, pointing to the crew chiefs and gunners. "We ran into Sadler here and had a drink."

"And I was doing some IP shit with Anderson," said De-Weiss. "We decided that we needed a drink and found you all here."

"Okay," said Anderson.

"Now that's providing anyone asks," said Sadler. "If they don't, we keep our mouths shut."

There was another commotion, but this one wasn't centered on the stage. Two men in civilian clothes entered. There was shouting at them because they weren't rated, men with wings. They were civilian employees from the embassy.

The noise radiated out from them, washing over the club like an incoming tidal wave. Silence fell with the wave, except for the shouting at the door. The music stopped, and the two women stood on the stage, wondering what had happened. Neither tried to get back into her clothes.

The voice of one of the embassy men carried into the room. "You've got to let me in," he shouted. "Really, you'll want to hear this."

"We won't stay long," said the other. "We're on official business."

"We've an announcement to make," said the first man.

The club manager worked his way through the crowd and demanded, "What in the hell is going on here?"

"These two sharpies want to make an announcement."

"Shit, is that all? Let them." He faced the men. "But make it quick, because we don't have all fucking day."

As the two men headed for the stage, the club manager retreated to his place behind the bar. When the men got to the stage, the women scooped their clothes from the floor, disappearing into the rear, out of sight.

One of the men held his hands up, as if asking for quiet. He stood there until the buzz of conversation died, then said, "We've run into a bit of a problem tonight."

"Big fucking deal."

"No, now listen. In the last hour or so, a dozen formal protests have been filed with the American embassy and the government here in Saigon by the Cambodian government and the North Vietnamese. It seems that one of the enemy's strongholds on the other side of the border was attacked by a squadron of U.S. helicopters."

There was a moment of silence and then sudden, wild cheering. Men were dancing in the aisles, screaming and shouting and laughing and slapping each other on the back.

On the stage, the man held his hands up, trying to silence the crowd. He glanced at his partner, who shrugged helplessly.

When it was quiet again, the man said, "It was an unsanctioned, illegal act of the worst kind."

"Bullshit."

The man laughed and said, "Well, that's the official line, but between you and me, the unofficial line is that it's about time. Unofficially, I think some of our people would like to give medals out."

There was more cheering and then someone started to chant, "Buy the bar! Buy the bar!"

The man stood there, shaking his head slowly as if he couldn't believe that the conduct of the war was being left in the hands of such an immature group. When it quieted again, he said, "If anyone has any knowledge of who did this, we'd like to know it."

"Right. You're the first people we'd tell."

"Seriously," said the man, "an investigation into the incident is being launched. Anyone with information is asked to contact the American embassy, or the CID office at USARV. Thank you for your time."

"Buy the bar!"

Anderson leaned forward and sad, "Christ, an investigation."

"Don't sweat it," said Sadler. "All the evidence, if there is any, is in Cambodia, and there's nothing to link us to the helicopters. They can link our unit, but not us. Besides, how hard are they going to investigate? Secretly, they're going to be rooting for us. Unless we get stupid, this thing is going to blow over in a couple of weeks."

"If you've finished your beer," said Wilde, "we'd better head back. Don't want to get into trouble for being off the base drinking in Saigon."

Two weeks later the official investigation was closed when no one could identify the pilots or the unit they had come from. Major Fox, not wanting to look stupid, listed his missing aircraft as destroyed in combat, and it was replaced two days later. He failed to investigate the disappearance, feeling that a new helicopter was better than a mountain of paperwork explaining where the old one went.

Three weeks later, Anderson received his AC orders, finding that it wasn't that much different than flying as a PPIC, except that everyone assumed that he knew more than he did.

He celebrated the occasion by buying the bar at the Gun-fighter's Club and getting so drunk that it was two days before he could be scheduled to fly, and there was some discussion about rescinding his orders on the grounds of bad judgment.

That didn't happen.